MAXSON HUNT

The Path (Clean)

This novel is entirely a work of fiction. The names, characters and incidents portrayed in it are the work of the author's imagination. Any resemblance to actual persons, living or dead, events or localities is entirely coincidental.

First edition

ISBN: 978-0-578-99000-2

This book was professionally typeset on Reedsy.
Find out more at reedsy.com

Contents

Prologue

Officer Neil Guerro sat at his desk in the precinct of Miami PD. He was new on the force and had been quickly shuffled to Night shift desk duty. He wasn't sure who he had pissed off to earn this wonderful new position. But he was going to take this position as seriously as possible. Especially because the precinct had been a buzz lately with all of the deaths. His job was to monitor the security cameras, of which there were a lot. It took him roughly 2 minutes to cycle through all of the cameras and come back to the start. He had just finished his loop and was beginning again. He looked at his watch, *Only 11 o'clock pm, this night is just going to drag on.* Neil began yet another loop of the cameras. About halfway through his cycle, Neil noticed something that wasn't there before. He wasn't sure what he was seeing, but he thought it might be a box. That was peculiar. Neil was sure that it wasn't there the last time he cycled through the cameras. He paused the footage and started rolling it back. About 30 seconds earlier in the footage, a figure just off camera slid the box into view and disappeared. Neil noted the time stamp and then cycled through the rest of the cameras to see if there was a better angle. However, even with all of the cameras, he didn't see who had dropped off the box, or where it came from. One of the street cameras caught just a glimpse of a black SUV rolling by the camera. But the windows were as solid black as the car, and it had no distinguishing marks, and no license plate. Now he started to worry. Neil picked up the radio and asked if any of the patrol units were at the precinct. The reply was less than proper procedure, "Yah Neil, It's Brad, I am pulling in the parking lot right now."

Neil responded, " Unit 74 please use proper protocol. There is something in parking quadrant 4 South. Can you please check and advise."

Neil waited patiently for the reply, He heard the radio come to life, and heard a sigh come across. " 74 responding."

Neil watched on the cameras as Brad rolled across the different parking lots to where the mysterious box was. Brad got out of his patrol car, and carefully walked towards the box.

Neil watched as Brad walked up and without hesitation and opened the box. Then he heard the radio, "Uhhh Neil, you are going to have to get the Captain on the phone, there is a body in this box. And what appears to be a note sitting neatly on top."

* * *

6 Days Earlier

Brenda Stone loved living in Miami. Where she and her husband had decided to retire was one of the nicer places in town, and they had been there for almost two years, and not one police siren was ever heard. Her Husband Neil had taken some convincing to buy a house in Miami. He had said that he would never live in Miami proper. But she always got her way. Neil was already in bed, but she couldn't sleep, so she was just sitting in her recliner watching a TV show.

Brenda was about to fall asleep when she heard a tire screech down her road. *That's quite peculiar*, she thought. It was right about 11 Pm and there was a tire screeching down the road. She got out of her chair and decided to look out her window. She was going to see if she could see a license plate so she could report them to the police. When she looked out her window, she saw 4 larger vehicles in front of the house of her neighbor. *What was her name again?* She thought. "Ah yes, it's Kari." She said out loud. Brenda had met her once or twice. She seemed sweet. The four large vehicles was out of the ordinary though. So she decided to call 911 for no other reason than to report the vehicles for being loud.

The phone line rang for a very brief moment, "9-1-1, What's your emergency."

"Yes, I would like to report a car for being much too loud in my neighborhood."

"Ma'am, there is a non-emergency line that you can call with those sorts of things. Would you like the number."

"Well no, I would like you to take the report. This is an emergency, there are four large black vehicles in front of my neighbors house and they made a lot of noise when they pulled up."

There was a pause on the line.

"Ma'am, what did you say your address was again."

Brenda gave the operator her address, and there was a long pause. As Brenda watched, she saw the people come back out to their vehicles with a child kicking and screaming.

"It looks like the people are trying to take a young boy." Brenda said.

The 9-1-1 operator seemed to get much more stern.

"Ma'am, please stay inside your house. Police are on their way."

Brenda sat there and watched as the vehicles took off, and thought *There goes the neighborhood.*

CHAPTER 1

John was always a happy man. He never really got into much trouble. However, being a detective had its downsides, and John had found the single greatest downside of all.

On this particular night John was in a great mood. He finally found the link that would help ensure Frank "The Crusher" Johnson would be sitting in prison for a very long time. As John sat at his favorite bar "Cuffs", he thought about what a silly name "The Crusher" was. See he was called the crusher because, for some reason, his favorite means of disposal was a car crusher. John had been intrigued by this. How was it possible that a man like that was able to get away with disposing bodies in this manner? Well it seems, he was very good at covering his tracks. The entire whole of Miami PD knew he was guilty. Yet somehow could never get any dirt on him. John was the third detective to go undercover and try to gain enough intel to take down his operation. The previous two detectives did not fair too well. Miami PD had a knack for sending in new detectives for this sort of work, and it never fared well. In fact, more than one lawsuit had been brought against Miami PD for this oversight.

However, John was no rookie, he had 15 years on the job. 15 years of catching criminals, and putting them in cells. He was still great at it. At one point in time the CIA had tried to recruit him. Having been born in Belle Glade, a town of less than 20,000 people. He wasn't much for the huge city life. Miami was the biggest city he had ever lived in and he was not about to move to DC for some job. John had contacts all over, and after 9 months with Frank, he eventually found the link he was looking for. A fingerprint in the vehicle that he had recently crushed with a rival inside.

John thought about the words that Frank said as they hauled him away. "YOU WILL PAY FOR THIS JAKE!!" He had screamed past the officer putting him in the backseat of his cruiser. He hadn't even known his real name.

"John, you okay there brother?". Crawling out of his thoughts he looked over at his partner. His partner, Kyle, was a tall man, about 6' 3", and roughly 250 lbs. He had a dark beard that was well trimmed and made him look like Jason Mamoa. His hair was as black as night, and he kept a very straight cut. He had come out of the military, so he never really liked long hair. He was built like a brick wall, and had arms that were massive. "Yeah, I'm great" John said as he patted Kyle on the back. " Just got lost in thought that's all." Kyle looked at John and raised his glass, Don't you go ruining our ritual just because this one actually yelled at you." This ritual the Kyle spoke of was pretty simple. Every time one of them closed a big case, they would head on down to "Cuffs" and get a double of Tulamore D.E.W.. This ritual was sacred to them, they had been doing this since they closed their first case together almost 10 years ago.

"You're right, I'm sorry." John said, holding up his glass. "To yet another criminal taken off the streets."

"Here, Here," Kyle said, tapping his glass against John's.

After about an hour at the bar, John and Kyle said goodbye. Getting to his car, a pearl blue Dodge Challenger. This was John's dream car. He had bought it about 9 months ago after saving for it for nearly a year. This car was decked out, he had blacked out wheels, which made this car look even meaner. As he hopped in the car, he dialed his wife with the Bluetooth calling feature. He was never one to drive without a hands free option. After a few rings, the phone went to voicemail, and the voice of his wife came across, like the voice of an angel. "Hey, you've got Kari's phone, leave a message, and I'll call you back when I get the chance." John listened through the options and after the beep, "Hey Gorgeous, you are probably asleep, but I am leaving cuffs now, and will be home in about 20 minutes."

On his drive home, he thought some more about Frank. *What did he mean by this threat?* He had many people threaten him in his 15 years, but this one rung home. Frank was a man not to be trifled with. He was the single biggest criminal that John had caught. And yet, he felt as if he had done something wrong.

Now about 11 PM John was cruising down U.S. Route 27, headed Northwest. He was about to pass the Chesapeake Motel when he saw the lights behind him. He looked down, and hadn't realized he was going almost 70 in a 40 MPH zone. He pulled over, and gathered his license and registration while the officer walked up to his car. Immediately he recognized him. It was the only cop in Miami PD that had a bone to pick with him. Officer Delgado was a stocky man. About 5'10" and roughly 220 lbs. Had very little facial hair and almost no hair on his head. Made him look like a bald George Lopez. As he walked up to the car, John rolled down his window.

"Evening Delgado," John looked up at him, "look my bad, I know I was speeding, I just wasn'-,"
     Delgado cut him off, "Sir, do you know what the speed limit is on this road?".

"Yes, I was just about to say -"

Delgado cut him off again, " Sir, have you been drinking?"

Now a little agitated, John said in an aggressive tone, "Look, just give me my ticket, and let me be on my way Delgado."

'Sir, please step out of the car, I have reason to believe that you've been drinking."

John got out of the car, now visibly irritated at Delgado. John had been drinking, but he could handle his liquor, a double of Whiskey wouldn't even touch him. See John was not a small person. He was 6'2", and roughly 230 lbs. He had a beard that wrapped around his chin and connected to both sideburns on his face. He didn't have a mustache, as he was never very good at growing one. Had a head of blonde hair, kept neatly trimmed. John had never been in the military but he never liked long hair. He grew it out one summer as a kid and it never sat well.

As Delgado proceeded to waste 10 minutes of his time on various field sobriety tests, John thought some more about Frank. Frank knew him as Jake Huston, a hired bodyguard. A very good hired bodyguard. In the 9 months John worked on him, John had become one of Frank's most trusted advisors. He would help him with the day to day of being a drug lord. Frank had begun to trust "Jake", far more than he trusted others. He even let him meet his wife. John felt it was going to be rough once he finally closed on him. He had broken bread with the man. Met his family, knowing full well what he was going to be doing to that family once he was done. This hit a little close to home. John had a 4 year old at home. His boy hadn't seen him in weeks. He had to go without seeing his son for the role of "Jake". John was not a man to involve his family in the undercover roles. If he had to involve a family, he would always have a backup family, a female detective he worked with and an 18 year old boy that looked like he was 15.

His wife Kari was always comforted by the fact that he always came home to her. John would always stare into her blue starburst eyes and reassure her that he would come home. That was one of the things that John loved most about Kari. He could stare into her eyes for hours. Kari was a beautiful woman. She was roughly 5'3" and 128 lbs. Being a Pilates instructor she was very fit. Had blonde hair with a hint of red in it that just added to her beauty. She would often wear her hair up, but he loved when she wore it down and curled.

When her hair was styled like this, it accentuated her face in such a way that he couldn't take his eyes off of her. Whenever he came off an assignment, he would go home and envelope her in a hug for hours. He missed her dearly all of his time away, as she missed him. But they both understood what he did for a living. And as long as he always came home, she was okay with it.

His Boy, Lane, was always happy to see him. John was so excited to go home and see his little boy. He was almost 4 foot tall. John couldn't believe how big the boy was getting. He had the same starburst eyes as his mother. Same Reddish blonde hair, and an attitude to match. Lane was a feisty kid that was always trying to wriggle his way out of trouble. His chubby little face would wrinkle when he wouldn't get his way. John thought this was absolutely adorable. Which would make it hard to discipline Lane without a smile on his face.

After the 10 minute field sobriety check, and a breathalyzer, Delgado angrily let him go with a ticket for 75 in a 40. John knew he wasn't going that fast, but he didn't want to argue with Delgado, he just wanted to get home to his wife, now 15 minutes later than he wanted.

John's house was a simple 3 bedroom 2 bath house in Miami Springs Florida.
    His house wasn't a mansion but it had been perfect for him and Kari when they bought it, just before Lane was born. His house was a Grey house with a round about driveway and a 2 car garage.

As John pulled up to the house, he knew something was off. His garage door was open, and Kari's car wasn't there. She never left the house this late, and whenever she left the house, she always closed the Garage door. As he pulled into the garage something didn't feel right. He quickly got out of the car and ran into the house. When he got inside, he knew something was wrong, his living room was torn to pieces, and all of the lights were on. This looked like some sort of robbery. When he walked into the house he had yelled Kari's name hoping for a response. When he did not get one, he started to panic. As he ran down the hallway, he noticed all of the doors open, when he got to his bedroom his entire world froze.

There on the bed, was his wife, covered in blood. As he ran to her, he could see that she was still alive, barely holding on. His tunnel vision kicked in and she was his sole focus. She had been stabbed twice in the stomach, just below the diaphragm. He immediately grabbed the sheets to try to stop the bleeding. She turned to him "H..hello love". As she spoke she started to cough. Coughing up blood, she looked into John's eyes. "They took him." She said, "They took my baby."

John's heart stopped, he wasn't sure he had heard that correctly. Then Kari repeated herself," Th.. they took.. they took Lane." As she finished her sentence she again coughed, this time wheezing. John was now in tears. Holding his dying wife in his arms, knowing there was nothing he could do. Many years on the job have given him the knowledge that she wouldn't survive. He held her to his body and said," Who took him?"

As she was taking her last breaths, she said, " F... Frank."

After uttering the name, John watched Kari's eyes roll back, and felt her body go limp. He was so stricken, he couldn't move. He just held onto Kari's body tightly as tears ran down his face.

Then he heard the sirens, as he sat there holding onto the lifeless body of his soul mate, the woman that meant everything to him. Cops started pouring into the house. As they came into the bedroom, they saw John there, holding Kari, tears streaming down his hardened face.

One in particular walked up to him, as John looked up, he saw the face of Delgado. The moment John saw Delgado, he snapped. In the very moment he saw him, he blamed him. He knew that he was to blame. Not that the man actually killed his wife, but that he had delayed him enough time, that he wasn't able to save his wife.

With speed that no one was expecting, John lunged across the room and tackled Delgado. As Delgado hit the floor John screamed, "THIS IS YOUR FAULT." John started swinging, fists hard as iron, the first contact instantly knocked out Delgado. With the second swing, Grey face made a sound, the entire room heard an audible "Snap." John had just broken Delgado's cheek bone. As he drew back for the third swing, the officers around John grabbed him and hauled him away from Delgado.

As they pulled John away, he kept screaming, "IT'S YOUR FAULT!!" He must've said it 4 or 5 times before the police officers were able to calm him down enough to stop his yelling. At which point he then broke down into more tears.

Moments later Kyle ran into the room, shoving people out of the way. Seeing Kari's body on the bed, he instantly went to John. As he embraced john, he could feel him clawing to get past.

"What did he do to you?" Kyle asked

Through tears John looked at him and said "It's his fault!"

Kyle, knew that Delgado may be an asshole, but he was no killer. He grasped John on the shoulders and shook him slightly. "What did he do to you?"

John, still sobbing, just shook his head and put it in his hands.

As John continued to sob, Kyle realizing something was missing asked John, "Where's Lane?"

When Kyle said the name of his son, John's heart skipped a beat. At the sight of his wife he had lost it. He didn't even pay attention to what his wife had said. "They took him."

John then looked up at Kyle with a broken look in his eyes. Through tears, John mumbled" F..Frank too-.." Choking back tears, John continued, "Frank took him."

The color drained from Kyle's face. He knew it was entirely possibly, but he hoped that John wasn't right.

CHAPTER 2

After a few minutes Kyle was able to get John out of the house, to give Miami PD a chance to clean everything up.

Kyle put John in the car and drove towards the station. On the way to the precinct Kyle started to question John on what had happened. "I am so sorry man. What happened?"

John had begun to calm down into a quiet stupor, still with tears streaming down his face. " I don't know man." John threw his hands in the air and shrugged his shoulders. " You know everything I know."

Kyle could tell that he was not going to get any more info out of John, and if he pried anymore, John would likely explode in anger. The rest of the ride to the precinct was silent. Kyle felt there wasn't anything he could do to console John. After all he had just watched his wife die in his arms.

Arriving at the precinct, Kyle urged John to go into the building so they could try figure out what happened. John just shook his head and looked blankly into the distance. Kyle could see that what John had been through had broken him. Kyle ultimately decided that he would sit in the car with John until he was ready to come into the precinct. As Kyle sat there with John in silence he couldn't bring himself to ask John any further about what had happened. He also had a feeling that John had told him everything he knew.

CHAPTER 3

Somehow John was able to doze off in the passenger seat of Kyle's Mustang. However, it was not a restful sleep. It was haunted by nightmares, nightmares of what he had seen. He was startled awake by the sight of his deceased wife covered in blood. When he awoke, it was about 3 am. The Miami PD precinct looked like a ghost town. There was a haunting fog that had rolled in off the water. John quietly got out of Kyle's car so he would not wake him. He was not in any better shape, but he knew what he had to do. He had to get his son back at all costs. He was not about to let Frank get away with murdering his wife.

John knew that it was not Frank who had wielded the knife, but he was definitely behind it. Frank was going to be his first stop. But first he had to get past the night shift. They had undoubtedly heard about what happened. They would have orders to keep him out of Frank's cell.

All inmates were kept in the holding cell on floor 2 before being transferred to the prison they would be held at. Since Frank had just been taken into custody that afternoon, it was a likely first stop.

As John entered the station he was greeted by the officer on duty at the front desk. Jackson was usually the officer on duty at the front desk. He was a cop that had put in 29 years. He loved working the night shift and was always dressed to a T. Being a more stocky build he was suited for the role. Officer Jackson had many years of desk duty and doughnuts under his belt. Ever since he had hip surgery he hadn't been able to chase down a criminal.

Shaking out of his thought John said, "Hey Jackson, just going in to grab some things."

"No can do big haus, I'm under strict orders not to let you in without an escort."

John knew what that meant, Frank was in the building.

"I know you are trying to follow protocol, but Kyle is right behind me. He was just shutting off the car." John gave Jackson the most convincing look he could.

"You know John, just because I like you, I am going to let you in. Kyle better be right behind you."

John looked at Jackson and held his hand up and shook his head back and forth." Scouts honor."

As John walked briskly into the precinct he felt bad for lying to Jackson, but he had to have his chance with Frank. As he reached the elevator, John thought about what he was going to say to Frank. He wasn't even sure he was going to have the courage to go through with this.

As the doors opened on the second floor, he could tell that almost everybody had gone to his house. The rows of cubicles were empty. Not a soul in sight. *I wonder where all the guards are at?* He thought as he wandered past the empty cubicles. After passing the cubicles he turned right to go towards the holding cells. This precinct of Miami PD didn't house long term criminals. Usually anyone that was brought in was processed and sent to the Main jail house to await trial or post bail. The precinct only had about 12 cells. One of which was essentially a drunk tank. It held about 12 people at once.

In the far back of the room was where they would keep the most dangerous criminals. It was the hardest area to penetrate, and had best surveillance.

As John walked up, he noticed frank on the cot, sleeping soundly. John slowly opened the cell door and walked towards Frank. Seeing how peaceful Frank was, just sitting there without any care in the world. He snapped. John grabbed Frank by the legs and threw him onto the floor. Now Frank was not an extremely large person. He was about 5'11" with a medium build. He liked to work out, but he was not as fit or strong as one might initially think.

When John yanked Frank out of his cot and onto the floor, Frank woke up, and was not happy about it. After realizing what was going on, Frank tried to get up quickly. However, John had seen Frank fight and knew how to take him down. John stomped on Frank's right knee. Ever since Frank had surgery on it, his right knee had been a weakness to him. After stomping on Franks right knee, John got over Frank and started to throw punches.

While continuing to punch, John screamed, "WHERE IS HE?"

Instantly John could see the glimmer of evil in Frank's eye, "I Haven't the foggiest idea." Grinning through blood on his lips Frank said, "I'm not even sure what you are talking about."

The Grin that was on Franks face broke John, he started swinging again, landing blows left and right. Right about that moment John felt Kyle grab him and haul him off of Frank. Kyle threw John into the hallway and followed suit. He then closed the cell door to Frank's room before Frank was able to get off the floor. However, Frank soon was at the door, laughing maniacally, he yelled, "I'll have your job for this... JOHN!!"

Hearing the words come out of Frank's mouth, Kyle knew that he was responsible for Kari's Death, and Lane's kidnapping. But attacking Frank was not the way to get answers.

"John, what are you thinking?" Kyle motioned towards the cell as he said this.

"Kyle, I don't expect you to understand, but HE.." John threw his arm outward towards the cell. "He is responsible for everything, and I WILL do everything it takes to find Lane."

John got up and got in Kyle's face,"Now either get out of my way, or lock me up. But nothing, and I mean NOTHING, will keep me from beating him to death to find my son."

Knowing full well that he would not stop, Kyle grabbed John and quickly cuffed him. "Look John, I understand you want to find your son, and I know he is responsible, but beating him to death is not going to solve anything. You get me?" Kyle had put his right hand on John's shoulder.

"Don't touch me Kyle." John quickly moved his shoulder so that Kyle's hand was no longer on it. "I can't believe you are taking HIS side."

Kyle Grabbed John by the arm and pushed him down the hallways. "I'm not taking sides, I am just trying to keep you alive and employed."

"Whatever..." John began to shut down again. As he walked in front of Kyle, he thought about the way that Frank had said his name. He knew exactly who he was. He must've known longer than he let on. Which would beg the question, why didn't he come after him sooner. Just outside the holding area was a group of 5 interrogation rooms. Kyle quickly pushed John into one and sat him in a chair. He then took his hands and cuffed him to the table.

"Look man, I am sorry to have to do this, but I can't have you killing our number one suspect. You are going to sit here until Cap arrives."

CHAPTER 4

Sitting in the interrogation room, watching the minutes slowly tick by, John started to calm down. He knew what he went into the cell to do, but when he saw him there, sleeping peacefully, he lost it. As he waited, he felt relieved that Kyle had stepped in when he did. If it wasn't for Kyle, John knew that he most likely would've killed Frank. John felt he needed to apologize to Kyle, he had been very hostile towards him, but he hoped Kyle knew that it was just a product of being near Frank.

"John, John save me!" John heard the voice of his beloved. "John, you didn't save me." As John looked around, the room was dark, except for his wife. She was illuminated by some light that he couldn't make out. Holding the wounds in her abdomen. John could see the blood pouring out of her. He tried to make his way towards her, but he couldn't move. As he finally broke free from what was holding him he stumbled and fell towards the ground. "KARI!" John snapped awake. This was the nightmare he had been having in the car. Why wouldn't it go away? Looking up, John saw the time on the clock. He had been asleep for almost an hour. The time read 5:15.

A few minutes later, Captain Hormel came into the room. Captain Hormel wasn't excessively tall, but he looked like he could bench the weight of a small car. His chest and arms were so massive he had earned the nickname " Gorilla." He was really, quite nice, but had the temper of a Don't touch Gorilla. As Hormel entered the room, John saw the anger in his eyes. As Hormel adjusted his glasses, John said, "Look Cap, I'm s—." Hormel quickly cut him off. " I don't give a shit if you are sorry or not. Your little attack has made a storm that I get to clean up." Hormel waved his hand in the direction of the cells. As the captain walked towards the other side of the table, John started again. "I know I messed up, but I just lost it."

Captain Hormel sat down in a huff. "Look John, I realize why you did it, and coming in here today, I wanted to do the same thing. But killing HIM...," again Hormel threw his arm in the direction of the cells. "Is not going to solve a damn thing. In fact it will probably make things worse."

Hormel continued, "You know you weren't supposed to go in there. Hell, you weren't even supposed to come into the precinct." Hormel motioned towards John, "Now I have no choice but to suspend you." Hormel paused, John could tell this was difficult for him. "Starting today, you will be on minimum one month suspension." Hormel opened his palm and motioned towards John. "I am going to need your badge and your gun."

John slowly handed over his badge and his gun. He knew this was not the Captain's fault. John knew that he was lucky to still have a job. "I understand Cap."

As Hormel took away the items he again motioned at John, "Because I like you, you are getting suspended with pay." Hormel paused to gain his thoughts. "But pull any of this shit again, and you may not have a job."

Captain Hormel got out of the chair, and walked towards the door. When he got to it he said, "Oh, and DO NOT, under any circumstances come to the precinct while you are on suspension."

John quickly acknowledged him "Yes Sir!"

As Hormel walked out of the office, John heard him grunt loudly at Kyle, "Go uncuff him."

"And get him the hell out of here."

A few moments later, Kyle came into the room. "Look, I'm sorry John."

John looked at Kyle as he was uncuffing him. "Hey man, no need, thank you for keeping me from killing him."

After uncuffing John, Kyle walked towards the door. "Hey, no problem man. I know you would do the same to me."

John and Kyle walked past the rows of still empty cubicles. John didn't expect to see anyone in yet, usually the day crew came in around 7. And the night crew came into the precinct about 6:15 to fill out paperwork and get ready to leave. For the most part, the cubicles went unused during the night.

As they got into the elevator Kyle said, "You should apologize to Jackson. His ass is getting suspended because he let you in. His suspension is only for 2 days though."

John felt a twinge of guilt. He hadn't wanted to get Jackson in trouble, but he needed to get into the precinct. When the elevator doors opened, John walked briskly down the hallway. Getting to Jackson's desk, John said, "Hey Jackson, sorry you got suspended too. That was never my intention."

Jackson looked up from the computer screen. "No need for an apology John, I knew what you were going to do, and I let you in because he deserves it. I'm just glad I was able to get Kyle up there before you did too much damage."

John scratched his head, "I was wondering how he knew I was in there."

Jackson motioned towards the computer screen, "It was really quite satisfying to watch you beat on him. But don't worry, the camera's mysteriously weren't working at the time." Jackson winked at John.

That briefly made John smile, he knew without the tapes, that Frank wouldn't be able to use his attack to get out. At best he would only be able to get transferred to another jail. John held up his fist, "Thank you."

Jackson smiled and knocked his fist against John's, "I've always got your back."

John and Kyle walked out of the building and go into Kyle's car.

As Kyle pulled out of the parking lot of the precinct, John pointed to the right. "Go that way."

Kyle looked slightly confused, and said, "What is that way?"

When John looked back at Kyle, Kyle could see the intensity in his eyes. "The storage unit."

CHAPTER 5

Kyle had instantly known what John meant. There was a storage unit off the Wharf that the two of them had gotten. This was no ordinary storage unit. It housed close to $100,000 in firearms and equipment. In the ten years they were partners, they had continually made deposits to this storage unit. They wanted the stockpile in case it was ever necessary to have an arsenal. This made Kyle nervous. But he knew that he was not going to talk John out of it. And even if he had stopped him from going at that time, he knew he could not keep John out of it. They had made it to where either of them could get into it without the other. There were also precautions taken so that they could never be locked out of it.

"John, that is a bad idea." Kyle knew he wouldn't be able to talk him out of it but had to try.

John, still looking at Kyle with a look that scared Kyle. "Did it sound like I was asking for an opinion?" John blinked slowly, "I am doing this with or without you. Your choice."

Kyle didn't like the sound of that but knew he would never forgive himself if he didn't help. "Fine, but we need a plan."

As they drove towards the Wharf, John and Kyle discussed their plan of attack. First they had to figure out exactly who took Lane. They knew that Frank was behind it, but Frank had his hands in a lot of pockets. He had an empire, and they knew they would have to start at the bottom.

On the way there, Kyle took a few unnecessary turns to make sure they weren't being followed. This storage unit is not something they could risk getting into the wrong hands. John did not like wasting time, but he understood the necessity.

Arriving at the storage yard, both Kyle and John looked around before getting out of the vehicle. They walked up to the unit and used the hidden fingerprint sensor to unlock the doors. As the doors swung open, some lights were activated and lit up the Unit. The Storage unit was the biggest one they could find. It was actually several units put together. The entire floor space was 30' x 30'. It looked like a well organized 3 car garage. There were rows of locked racks, as well as guns on every wall. There must have been well over 100 guns in the unit. Most of the guns were on the walls, while all of the ammo was locked in the well organized racks. There was enough firepower to support a small militia. Well over 500,000 rounds of ammunition in all calibers. There were also a wide selection of combat weapons. There were swords, knives, throwing knives, nun chucks, and even a flail.

John instantly walked up to where the nun chucks was resting. This rifle was chambered in 7.62x51 NATO. It had an adjustable power scope that had a magnification range of 5x - 25x. John had practiced with this rifle many times. He was damn near a master, and he knew it. After grabbing the rifle, he walked over to where the assault rifles rested. There were many to choose from, but John's favorite was the M416. This military grade assault rifle was the most reliable in the bunch. He had a 4x magnification scope on it, with canted iron sights. This made the weapon a great choice for short or long range. Last but not least, John grabbed a pistol. This was not a hard choice at all. John's most trusted handgun was the M1911. Although it was a remake it was as close to the original as possible. The 1911 shot a .45 ACP round. He had this gun equipped with upgraded tritium sights.

While John was packing up, Kyle grabbed a few guns that John was not paying attention to. However John knew that Kyle would also opt for the 1911. They had discussed this firearm at length.

After loading all of the ammunition into the trunk of the mustang, the two of them locked up the unit and got in the car.

As they got in the car, Kyle turned to John. "There is no coming back from this, are you sure you want to go down this road."

The answer Kyle got was expected. "Drive the car Kyle. We are doing this."

CHAPTER 6

Both Kyle and John knew the first place to start was the bottom. They weren't sure who Frank would have hired, but they were not going to rest until they found out.

They agreed that their first stop should be "Shakes." He was one of their criminal informants. He got the nickname from being strung out on Heroin. Once he stopped using, "Shakes" was one of their better CI's. He had a lot of contacts and was always willing to help.

When they arrived at "Shakes'" house, he was out front tending to a garden that helped him stay sober. The moment he saw the Mustang, he ran inside and locked the door. Kyle looked over at John, "Why don't you let me take this one."

John glared back at Kyle, "Not a chance."

After they got out of the car. John ran up to the house. He knocked once, followed by," Shakes, either you open this door or I kick it in. Your choice."

John paused a moment, he did not have any patience to be tried. He stepped back, and as he got ready to kick the door, he heard the lock click. Then he heard a shaky voice, "Please man, just leave, I don't want any trouble."

Kyle got to the door and tried the knob. "Shakes it's me, Kyle, I'm coming in." He turned the knob and opened the door. Before he could finish opening the door, John rushed past him and shoved "Shakes" against the wall. "Shakes" thudded against the wall and put his hands up to keep John from hitting him. Instead of taking a swing, John pushed his hands away and put his forearm against "Shakes'" neck.

"Who took my son?" John asked this with such ferocity, that it startled Kyle. "I.. I don't know man." "Shakes" responded hesitantly. This only served to further frustrate John.

At this point John pushed against "Shakes" so hard he was lifting him by his neck. "I'll only ask one more time, Who.." John pushed even harder against "Shakes'" throat that he couldn't breathe. "WHO took my son?"

John let "Shakes" go so he could respond. Coughing, "Shakes" said, "Man, I don't know who took him." He cowered and held up his hand."But... but I know someone who might know."

John helped "Shakes" off the floor. "What's his name."

"Not HIM, Her. She is a high end prostitute that works on most of Frank's crews. She listens to these guys blab on about all of the shit Frank has them do."

"Shakes" dusted himself off. "Her name is Precious. I can call her and set up a meeting, but she only shows up for money."

"Shakes" pulled his phone out of his pocket and dialed a number. "Hey girl, how are you?"

John and Kyle couldn't hear the response.

"Shakes" continued, "I have a new client for you, lots of cash to waste, wants to meet up tonight."

"Perfect he will see you there, name is John." He hung up the phone. "All right guys. She will be at the Marriott at Biscayne Bay. Room 501. 8 pm sharp." "Shakes held up his hand. "She does not respond well to late arrivals."

John patted "Shakes" on the back rather hard. "See now was that so difficult?"

Leaving the house Kyle grabbed John's elbow, "You almost killed him dude. You going to do the same thing to Precious?"

John thought about his response for a moment. "I know, but right now, I am going to do anything to get the information I need." John opened the door to the Mustang and got in the car before Kyle had a chance to respond.

After Kyle got in the car, he looked at John, "Even if that means killing an innocent guy?"

John craned his neck slightly, "Innocent, you want to talk innocent?" John glared at Kyle, "My WIFE was innocent, My SON is innocent. That drug dealer inside that house, he is not innocent by any means. He may not have had anything to do with what is going on, but he is NOT innocent."

Kyle began to apologize, "Look I'm sorry ma—." John cut him off before he could finish, and grunted, "Just drive the car."

The drive to the Hotel was done in silence. Kyle knew he had misspoken and did not want to risk angering John further. John was usually a level headed guy, but in this instance Kyle knew there was no reasoning with John.

When they arrived at the hotel it was just after 10 AM. John knew there was time he would need to wait but he wanted to make sure he was in the hotel and ready. Walking up the the front counter, John had a plan. He was going to ask to be put on floor 5. Where he would wait for Precious to show up. This way, he would be able to see anyone with her before the meeting.

CHAPTER 7

The hours seemed to drag by. John tried to take a nap, but there was no getting to sleep with those nightmares. Both John and Kyle were in the same room. Every time Kyle tried to talk to John, John would simply glare back at Kyle.

At about 2 PM John was able to break into room 501. He wanted to get inside and make sure he had backup in there in case anything went wrong. First thing he did was check for cameras and wiretaps, after about 15 minutes he felt the room was secure enough. The first thing John did was tape a pistol underneath the coffee table. This would ensure he would be able to get to a weapon in the main living area. He then went into the bedroom and tucked a 10 inch fixed blade under the bed. He had only brought one handgun, but he was sure he would be okay with a couple of knives stashed around the place. The only other place he thought he would need a weapon in was the kitchenette. However, in checking around he was able to find a knife block with a couple of random knives. He checked the room one more time to make sure it looked clean. Then he snuck out of the room and back down the hallway.

His room was 4 doors down on the right hand side of the hallway. If he needed to make an escape. After getting back to his room, John realized it was only 3:30. He still had over 4 hours until she was due to show up. John decided to take the rest of the time cleaning his guns. He slowly broke down the guns and cleaned each individual part. He knew he could keep himself pre-occupied for at least a couple of hours by taking care of this.

In total he had brought 4 guns. He had put the 9 millimeter handgun in the other hotel room. With him he had the 1911, the M24, and the M416. He started tearing down the 1911 first since it saw the most action. Taking the gun apart was very simple and not at all time consuming. This gun could be taken apart without any tools. John pulled the slide back slightly and took out the slide pin that held the slide on. Then he took off the slide and begun to clean the weapon.

After the 1911 he cleaned the M416, then the M24. Each took a bit more time than the handgun. After successfully cleaning and oiling all the weapons John had managed to burn about 2 hours. But he was getting antsy. Kyle was still sitting in the corner of the room quietly, just watching TV. John could tell that Kyle did not want to go through with this plan.

John stared at Kyle for a moment, "Hey Kyle."

Kyle looked up, "Hmm?" he asked inquisitively.

John scratched his head a bit, "Your guns need a cleaning too?"

Kyle chuckled lightly. "Nah man, why?"

After shaking his head, a rather uncomfortable John said, "I need to pre-occupy my mind somehow. You want to play some Gin Rummy?"

Kyle smiled softly, "Sure man, I'd love to."

Whenever Kyle and John needed to burn some time, they always played some Gin Rummy. It was a simple game and made the time pass by with far less discomfort. They even played on a few stakeouts. Though they had managed to ruin a few decks of cards playing in vehicles.

They passed the next couple hours playing cards. As the clock read 7:30 PM

John and Kyle finished up their last game. They then began to watch the hallway with the cameras they had placed there. After about 10 minutes they saw a rather gorgeous woman walking down the hallway. She was roughly 5'9" tall in the heels she was wearing. Her hair was a deep red that accentuated her face well. She was wearing a bit of makeup, but not too much. Across her lips was a dark red lipstick that matched her hair.

The dress she was wearing was a single strap that went down to about her mid thigh. It was a purple dress that was tight against her body and showed every curve. As she walked down the hallway, Kyle said, "She looks like Jessica Rabbit."

Behind her was a fairly tall gentleman, about 6'1", looking like he weighed about 270 Lbs. He was dressed in a black tux, and had a gun in his right hand. The woman was definitely Precious. John waited until she got into the room. He noticed that the man stopped and waited at the door. John thought momentarily about his next move. He didn't want the bodyguard around in case things went south with Precious. He ultimately decided to attempt to take out the bodyguard without killing him.

John looked around the room for something he could use to his advantage. He grabbed the bible out of the nightstand. This is how he was going to get close without the bodyguard getting too suspicious. Next John grabbed one of the towels from the bathroom. He had his plan set. John then let Kyle know what he planned to do.

He stepped out into the hallway with the towel draped around his neck and the bible close to his chest. He began to walk in the opposite direction as the bodyguard. The he stopped and put his head down, and thumped himself on the forehead with his palm. He turned around and started to walk back to the room. As he did he looked up at the bodyguard, who was only about 10 feet from him, and exclaimed, "I forgot my pool slippers!" Making a mocking face John then said, "I can be so stupid, I swear I'd forget my head if it wasn't attached."

This statement made the bodyguard chuckle slightly. He then said, "Hey man, I know what you mean."

At that moment John knew his plan would work. Shrugging, he held up the bible, "I don't usually do this, but have you found Jesus?"

The bodyguard looked skeptical, but he responded, " I go to Church almost every Sunday."

John smiled slightly, and paused for a moment, "... You look like you have had a rough day, could I pray for you?"

The bodyguard nodded, "I guess it wouldn't hurt."

John then motioned for him to come closed, "Come on over here, I like people to hold the good book with me while I pray for them."

The bodyguard paused for a moment, he looked like he wasn't going to do what John wanted. Then he looked at the door to the room precious was in and shrugged. "Alright." he said with a sigh.

As the Bodyguard walked over to John, he readied himself. John knew this was not going to be an easy task, and that if he made too much noise precious might hear him. John held out the bible for the Bodyguard to hold onto. Just before the man grabbed the book, John let it slip out of his hand. "Oh,.. Shoot." John quickly blurted out. The Bodyguard did exactly what he wanted and said, "I've got it." As the Bodyguard bent down to grab the book, John acted quickly. He grabbed the towel from around his neck, and with one motion he wrapped it around the Bodyguards neck and rolled over his back. After the roll John knelt down and pulled on the towel as hard as he could. The angle in which he had chosen to put the Bodyguard meant that his feel were behind him and he was bent backwards. This ensured that he had no leverage to regain control. John pulled hard on the towel. The Bodyguard struggle for a few second but realized he was not going to get out of this. After about 30 seconds of pulling tightly on the towel, he felt the man go limp.

Immediately Kyle opened the door to the room and helped John drag him in there. They both knew they had a very short period of time before the Bodyguard woke back up. They quickly cuffed his hands behind his back, and stuffed a rag in his mouth. They couldn't afford to have him screaming when he woke up.

John quickly got back up and went back into the hallway. John walked up, and using the key he just swiped off the Bodyguard he opened the door. When he stepped inside, he saw Precious sitting on the couch smiling.

Instantly John could tell that she knew her Bodyguard was no longer there for her. She chuckled slightly, "I have to hand it to you, whatever you did, you did it quietly. You didn't kill him did you?"

John wanted to try to play the game as long as he could. "What do you mean?"

She looked John up and down. "Don't lie to me, he always knocks 3 times and then lets people in. Always. If he didn't, that means you did something to him." She didn't look angry, she looked amused, so John went with it.

Smiling, John said, "He should be fine, and quiet is how I work."

Precious sighed softly, and made a wiping motion across her forehead. "Well that's a relief. It is so hard to find good help around here. Now you have exactly 2 minutes to tell me what you want before more arrive."

John didn't waste and time, he figured that her backup would be there in less than 60 seconds. "Name's Detective John Mauser. Now I assume by the name you know who I am, what I want to know is... Who.. Took.. My... Son." When he said his name, John saw the recognition flash across her face. As he asked his question, he saw her face turn white, and he instantly knew she had information.

Precious paused for a moment to think, and then looking quite frightened said, "I want protection, if I give you this information, they will kill me."

John thought about it for a moment, "I'll protect you as far as the Miami PD precinct, once you get inside, you should be safe 'till this is over."

Precious sighed, "Well if that is the best you have, then I guess I'll take it. Frank hired Gary Neitz to do whatever he did. I spoke to gary yesterday afternoon, and he said Frank paid him a lot of money to make sure you never forgot his name."

John recognized the name. Gary was the leader of Der Hass. A German biker gang that did a lot of work for Frank. They ran a big portion of Miami, and were not to be taken lightly. Although they had yet to be able to nail these guys for anything, Der Hass was credited with over 500 Kills in the last 4 years. Mainly members of rival gangs. But they did not discriminate. They would kill anyone for any reason, that is the reason they named themselves Der Hass, or *The Hate*. They had no love for anyone besides the men they rode with, and there was often killing among the group.

John knew he would have his work cut out for him. But nothing would stop him from getting his son, and getting revenge for his wife.

John looked at Precious for a moment, and thought about what to do. He waved to her, "Thanks doll, have a nice day."

Precious looked like she had been shot, She stammered, "What about my protection?"

John shrugged and said, "Blame it on your bodyguard, I don't personally care. But I am not protecting you. You knew something like this was going to happen, and you let it. You're as good as dead to me. The only reason I didn't kill you myself if out of respect for women. But whether or not you live is of no consequence to me."

John reached under the coffee table and grabbed the gun he had stashed there. He wasn't sure if he would have to shoot his way out or not. As he walked up to the door, he looked through the peephole. He did not immediately see anyone so he opened the door and ran for his room. As he was slipping into his room he saw the elevator door open, and he saw a man at the front of it with a submachine gun. He was not going to get out of this hotel without dropping some bodies. He quickly shut the door and motioned to Kyle.

Kyle jumped up and threw John his M416. They both looked at the monitor which was connected to the camera in the hallway. They counted 6 men. All of them holding what looked to be UMP's. A submachine gun capable of using 9MM, .40, or .45. However, most people used 9 MM because of the recoil. The gun was much more manageable in 9MM.

Without speaking, John and Kyle were on the same page. Kyle stood by the door, ready to open it. John motioned with his left hand. 3,... 2,....1. He then clamped his fist, at this exact moment Kyle opened the door, and John dove out of it firing the M416 almost immediately. Before he hit the ground he had hit two of the men in the forehead. The rest of the men scrambled to get their guns up. Before they could fire, Kyle stepped out of the room and squeezed off two rounds. Each hitting their target with accuracy. By this time the last 2 men in the hallway, had dropped their guns and were turning to run. John sat up and shot one in the right knee, and Kyle shot the second man about halfway up his back, dropping him instantly.

John turned towards the hotel room. "We just made a lot of noise, we need to leave. Now!"

Kyle nodded, "Agreed."

John and Kyle took less than a minute to gather everything up. They were prepared for this situation, so they made sure it would be easy to leave. They had connected to the Hotels security system, so before they left, they were able to remotely wipe the cameras for the entire time they were there. On their way down the hallway, John stopped at the man he had shot in the knee. The man was still in the same position, he had passed out out of agony. John reached down and slapped his face hard enough to make sure he would wake him. The man was barely conscious but John knew he wouldn't forget what he was told. "Tell Neitz that John Mauser is coming for him. And he isn't going to like it."

Then the two men went to the stairwell. They couldn't take the elevator and risk people seeing them. They proceeded to the ground floor, and left out the back entrance to avoid suspicion. They had parked Kyle's Mustang in a manner that made for an easy escape. Then they drove towards the Wharf again.

CHAPTER 8

Arriving at the Wharf again, they headed to the storage unit. As they were pulling up, they could both tell something wasn't right. They noticed a few cars near the storage unit. Kyle immediately stopped the car and put it in reverse. As he did, two men stepped out from behind one of the containers in front of them and began shooting at them. Kyle quickly accelerated in reverse and whipped the car around, threw it into first gear and drove around the containers. The bullets had hit the car, but not done much damage. Kyle had upgraded the windshield with level 3 Plexiglas. As well as upgrading the body panels with a fiberglass plating that was bullet resistant.

As they parked the car, they quickly got to the trunk and pulled out the two M416's they had. They still had plenty of ammunition. They each grabbed 3 magazines along with the guns. As well as the rifles, they each had their sidearm on them and carried 2 additional magazines for those.

Kyle and John could hear the men starting to advance. John grabbed one of the fragmentation grenades, pulled the pins and threw it around the containers at the men advancing. This was a tactic that both men knew well. As soon as the grenade exploded, one man, this time Kyle, looked around the corner and began shooting at the men. As he looked around the container, he saw 4 men. The closest one had taken damage from the grenade, and the other 3 were scrambling. He immediately took two shots at the men closest to him. He hit the man closest to him right between the eyes, putting him out of his misery. Taking the second shot he hit the man in the right shoulder but didn't stop him. By that time, the men had managed to get their weapons up and started shooting. He dropped back behind the containers.

While Kyle had peeked around the front of the containers, John had gone around the other side to catch them off guard. By the time the men had stopped shooting at Kyle, he had gotten far enough down to see the three men still standing. He stepped around the corner of the container he was behind and immediately started laying cover fire. His cover fire was less accurate than he usually was, but the idea was just to distract the men so Kyle could shoot them. However he still managed to hit the closest one to the containers, the same one Kyle had struck in the shoulder. Two of his bullets struck dead center, causing blood to spray in the direction of the other men. He instantly crumbled.

Upon hearing John's fire, Kyle stepped around the container and shot at the other two men that were scrambling from John's cover fire. One of the men was hit in the leg by a John, and was an easy target for Kyle. Putting two bullets in his chest, Kyle looked to the last man. He was starting to try and run, and Kyle shot him in the hip. The Idea was not to kill the last one. They needed one to interrogate.

Before they could get to the man however, they heard a shot ring out, and the last man was struck in the head.

Kyle yelled "SNIPER!"

As he did, he jumped back behind the containers that he had been standing behind. John had seen the direction of the blood splatter from the last man and quickly discerned that the shot had come from one of the shipping container cranes. But he was not sure which one. He was going to have to sprint across an opening and allow the sniper to shoot at him.

John Yelled, "Cover me!"

He then sprinted across one of the openings, and dove to the other side. As he did, he heard a shot ring out, and saw the concrete just to the left of him explode from the impact. Kyle had looked out the other side of the container as John did this and saw where the shot came from.

Kyle then called out, " South East 135."

Both men always kept a small compass on their rifles for this exact reason. John now knew the exact spot that the shooter was in. Kyle knew what to do next. He needed to distract the shooter for John, so he could take him out. Kyle was still by his car so he grabbed a concussion grenade out of the trunk. The next move had to be timed perfectly. He pulled the pin and yelled "Pin."

John knew what this meant. In exactly 5 seconds Kyle would throw the concussion grenade, in exactly 9 seconds, Kyle would then run out and dive towards it. What would happen is the shooter would scope in to shoot him, and the concussion grenade would temporarily blind him and allow John the precious time to shoot him.

John counted down, to himself 5...4...3...2...1..

He heard the grenade hit the ground, 3... 2... 1

John heard the concussion grenade go off, and stepped around the corner, scoped in to where the shooter was and saw that their plan had worked. Before the man could regain his aim, John squeezed the trigger. He saw the spray of blood from just below the man's neck. The bullet hit him with enough force that he lost his balance and fell 5 stories to the ground. If the shot hadn't killed him, the fall finished the job.

John ran over to where Kyle was. He wasn't hit by any bullets but he was still recovering from the concussion grenade.

John held out his hand, " Are you okay man?"

Kyle waved his hand, " I'm alright mate, those things hurt though."

He got up off the ground slowly. John had been on the receiving end of quite a few of the concussion grenades. He knew they weren't fun.

He patted Kyle on the back, "Good job man, that was a great call out."

As they walked towards the container, they noticed that the men that were there had tried to get into the container, but hadn't had much luck. "Looks like we got here in the nick of time." John said.

"We must have." Kyle agreed.

They were simply stopping by the storage unit to refill, and get a plan of attack. John needed to figure out where Der Hass was holding his son. Since he was undercover working for Frank, he knew a couple of the places where the members of Der Hass would spend their time. His first choice was a biker bar on the west side of town named, "Motorhead Bar and Grill." But most people just called the place Motorhead.

They were going to have to be tactful with how they approached this bar. At any given time there were about 20 members in there. After about an hour of going over plans the two of them agreed on a plan of attack.

CHAPTER 9

It took John and Kyle about 35 minutes to get to the other side of town. By this time, it was about 11 PM. There would be a lot of people at *Motorhead*, Derr Hass and otherwise. John decided it was best not to try to engage anyone inside the bar. Instead, him and Kyle had decided they were going to try to get one or two of the members outside alone. Preferably they were wanting to do this away from the bar, so more members wouldn't be attracted.

They sat outside the bar for about 15 minutes before seeing two men come out of the bar. Both wearing the patch that marked them as Derr Hass. The patch had a dark red background, with a Grim reaper holding a scythe across his body. In white lettering, the word Hass was stitched across the image. These were good men to interrogate. Both looked to be middle ranking. In his time undercover, John had learned that Derr Hass would stitch on images from chess to the bikers cut in order to discern the rank. Most members were either Pawns, or Rooks. These men were both Knights. This meant that they usually controlled part of town. They should have the information that John was looking for.

John and Kyle wanted to follow these men about a mile from the bar. But did not want them to get much further, and risk them noticing they were being followed. The plan was to follow them and then "accidentally rear end one of them at a stop sign or light. The two of them got ready, as they did not expect this to be an easy feat.

As they approached the stop sign, they heard a police siren behind them, and the lights came on. Kyle pulled over as the motorcyclists rode away. As he pulled the car to the side of the road, and shifted into park, he saw the officer get out of the car. Both John and Kyle knew this officer, it was Officer Gerand. Officer Gerand was what you expected a cop fresh out of the military to look like. He was almost 6 foot even. Whenever he talked about height, he exaggerated just a little, and said he was 6 foot. When in actuality he was 5'11".

Kyle rolled down his window, "What the hell are you doing Gerand?"

Gerand leaned in the window, "Boys, there's a Bolo out on you. The prostitute at the hotel, said you were the ones behind that hallway shooting. Captain Hormel wants anyone who sees you to bring you in. He knows what the two of you are up to."

John leaned towards the driver side of the car. "Listen Gerand, I can appreciate you doing your job, but you either let us leave, or we make you let us leave. One way or the other, we are not going back to the precinct."

Gerand took a moment to think about what he was going to say next. "John, I'm not here to take you in, I'm here to warn you. You need to get a new ride, fast. Every cop in the city is looking for this car. "

Kyle threw his hands up and pointed towards the bikes in the distance. "That was our best shot at not only getting a new ride, but some answers."

Gerand paused, " Follow me, we are going to get you those bikes."

They had to drive at about 120 MPH to catch up to the bikes. It did not take long at all at those speeds. When Gerand lit them up he instructed them to turn into a dark alley, and Kyle pulled in behind the cruiser with his lights off.

Gerand kept his siren on long enough for Kyle and John to get out of the car without the motorcyclists hearing them. As Gerand approached the bikers, John heard Gerand say, " Gentlemen do you know why I pulled you over tonight?"

"Obviously because you don't know who we are," one of the bikers scuffed.

He was a small man. Probably about 5'6" and weighing no more than 150 lbs. The other biker, however, John could see was not going to be easy. He was hulking. Even sitting on his motorcycle, he looked like he was at least 6 foot tall, and was easily 260 lbs.

The thin biker continued, "Can't you see the patch on the back of our cuts, *PIG!*." With that last word, you could hear this man's disdain for the police. After he said this sentence, he spat at Gerand's feet. Oddly enough, the hulking biker didn't seem to share this opinion. He reached out with an oversized hand and smacked the smaller biker hard enough to make him jot.

"Keep your stupid opinions to yourself, Blödmann." He said in a heavy German accent. He looked visibly upset at the smaller biker, who was now rubbing the back of his head. "Is there something we have done wrong officer?" The bigger biker said this in an almost confused tone.

"I am going to need to see some paperwork gentlemen. You were both going exceptionally fast for this area. The speed limit is 35. From my radar, I have both of you going at least 60. Also, your friend here, wasn't wearing a helmet." Gerand was just bullshitting his way through this traffic stop. However, from John's perspective, it looked like the bikers were buying it.

John was waiting for Gerand to find a reason to pull them off their bikes and bring them over to the hood of the cruiser. If he was able to do this, pulling off this feat would be a lot easier.

Both of the bikers had to get off of their bikes to pull out their paperwork. As with most motorcycles like these, the paperwork is kept in pouches that ride side saddle to the rear seat. Both the bikers handed their paperwork to Gerand at the same time.

"Thank you gentlemen, now if you wouldn't mind joining me over by the patrol car."

John could see that the smaller biker had started to say something, however, before a word escaped his mouth, the larger biker smacked him in the back of the head again. This time the hit was hard enough to make the smaller biker stumble forward.

"What did I say, *Boy*, keep your mouth shut." The biker had said the word boy, like he was disciplining a petulant child. As they walked toward the cruiser, the smaller made no more attempts to speak, occasionally shooting glances at the larger one.

"If both of you could please put your hands of the hood of the car. I'd like to frisk you for any weapons." As he spoke, Gerand motioned towards the hood of the car.

How was he doing this so well? John thought.

"Do either of you have any weapons you would like to declare before I begin?"

The larger one spoke first, "No Sir, is this really necessary though?"

John and Kyle were hanging back, so they couldn't quite see everything, but they heard the smaller one mutter something angrily. Before they could blink, the larger biker grabbed the back of the smaller one's head and slammed it into the hood of the police cruiser. His head hit the car with such force that it made an audible *Crack* sound.

At this new development, Gerand had pulled out his sidearm and pointed it at the biker.

"PUT BOTH OF YOUR HANDS ON THE HOOD AND DO NOT MOVE!" Gerand shouted the command with force. The larger biker let go of the back of the head of the smaller one. When he did, John could see that the hit had knocked the smaller one unconscious, and there was blood running down the hood of the car.

The larger biker complied with the demand and Gerand moved to put him in handcuffs. When he reached towards the bikers right hand, the biker moved to attack Gerand. Although this biker was very large, he was also extremely fast. He lifted his right hand and swung his fist toward Gerand like a backwards jab. Gerand was just fast enough to avoid getting hit by this biker. He quickly raised his Glock 22 and fired one clean shot. He did not move to kill the biker, he was just looking to incapacitate him. His shot tore through the bikers right shoulder. With the Glock 22 being chambered in .40 S.&W., it was not something that anyone would be able to shrug off. The Biker dropped to his knees and cursed. It was at this time John and Kyle deemed appropriate to join the fun. John walked up and put the end of his 1911 onto the back of the bikers head. "Don't even think about standing back up." John issues this statement with a growl. The tone was angry enough to garner a look from both Gerand and Kyle.

Kyle walked over to where the smaller biker was laying in a pool of blood. It was now clear that the impact with the hood had broken the bikers nose and knocked him unconscious. However, he was clearly still breathing.

John motioned for Gerand to come over and finish putting the biker in cuffs. After he had his hands cuffed behind his back, John grabbed the biker by his arm and hauled him up. The biker groaned as he did this. John had been shot before, so he knew it was not a pleasant feeling. He brought the biker over to a wall and turned him around so his back was facing the wall. Then he told the biker to sit against the wall. The biker looked at him as if he had asked him to do something completely unreasonable. John didn't like this response, he quickly moved forward, and brought his fist into the stomach of the biker. The biker was a large man, but John was even larger still. Everyone who knew John, also knew that it was not a good idea to be on the receiving end of his fists. The biker doubled over in pain from the impact. When he did, John shoved him down and the biker lost his balance and fell to his ass with his back against the wall.

Kyle then grabbed the unconscious biker and zip tied his hands together. Then he drug him over to the wall and set him next to the larger biker. John looked over to Gerand, "What is this asshole's name?" Gerand looked confused for a moment and then it clicked in his head that he had gotten their ID's. When he had pulled out his Glock, he simply dropped the ID's on the ground. He walked over to where they were laying and picked them up. He pulled out his flashlight and held it on his shoulder with his head. He looked over the cards momentarily.

"ID says, uhhh... Klaus Veitermen."

John looked back at Klaus who was still recovering from the jab to the stomach.

"Alright Klaus, I am going to ask you some questions, if you refuse to answer, or give me any lip, or if I think you are lying, you will be in a lot of pain. So, first question... are you going to answer any of my questions?" John knew that he probably hadn't intimidated Klaus enough for him to give any straight answers, and he was right.

"Eat shit and die, *Arschgesicht.*" This was the answer that John was hoping to receive, at this response, he pulled out the 7 inch blade that he had strapped to his side and plunged it into Klaus's left knee. Klaus showed obvious signs of pain, however, to his credit, John noticed that he did not scream. He simply grunted painfully. John couldn't help but be impressed by this. He had just stabbed this man in the knee with a rather large combat knife, and the man didn't even scream. He thought for a moment, and decided it might be easier to break the smaller biker. Who was barely conscious. He reached over and firmly slapped the smaller biker.

"Hey Gerand, What's this one's name?"

Gerand paused for a moment to look at the ID's again. "Looks like ID says Jack Nismuth."

John looked at Jack who was starting to wake up a bit more. "Say Jack, you feel like opening that mouth of yours to give me some information?"

Jack looked over at Klaus who was obviously in a lot of pain, but was not showing it very much. Klaus looked back at Jack with eyes that could pierce steel. Everybody noticed this look. It was a look that said, *If you say anything, I will kill you.*

"I - I am much more afraid of Klaus." Jack managed to say. Although it came out a little garbled as his nose was still broken and bleeding.

"Alright, look," John began, "I want to know where Gary took my son. I am going to kill whoever doesn't speak up first. And if neither of you are feeling very chatty, I will begin to carve you like a Thanksgiving turkey until you are feeling chatty." At this statement Frank grabbed John's arm, which was quickly pulled away.

Kyle motioned for John to step away from the men for a moment. "Hey Gerand, if either one of them moves, shoot them in the knee." Kyle said this matter of factly and grinned as he pulled John to the other side of the alley.

"Dude, I know what is at stake here, but you need to calm down." Kyle began in a hushed tone. "Killing people trying to kill us is one thing, but these men haven't attacked us in any manner. This is straight up assault and murder." Kyle put his hand on John's shoulder in a calming gesture. John jerked his shoulder free of Kyle's hand and looked him dead in the face. In an angry tone far from hushed John responded.

"I could care less about some piece of shit bikers. They work for Gary, and they are far from innocent. I would be doing the world a favor by killing them." John then pushed Kyle away and continued, "If you don't have the heart for this I will do it without you. But do not, I repeat do not try to talk me out of what is necessary to save my son." He paused only long enough to stare at Kyle through dead eyes that conveyed anger. "Or I will do the same to you."

Kyle knew not to push the subject any further, he did not want to give John cause to attack him as well. Knowing the state he was in, he knew it was more than a possibility if he stepped on his toes too much.

John walked back toward Klaus and Jack, a hint of a devious smile on his face. The kind of smile you would find on the devil before he carved you to bits. John walked over and in one swift motion he ripped the knife from its resting place in Klaus's knee, and thrust it towards Jack's neck. Only stopping the blade once it was firmly planted against Jack's neck. The plan was not to kill the man, but if he slipped at all, or Jack moved incorrectly, it will all be over for the small framed man. Jack had flinched when John had done this. It obviously was not something he was expecting, but it garnered the result John was looking for. John looked Jack directly in the eyes, their noses almost touching.

"If the next words out of your mouth are not telling me where I can find Gary, or agreeing to tell me, they will be your last." John said this in a tone not unlike a growling dog. Klaus decided this was the correct time to speak up.

"You— you tell him anything, and I will gut you like a pig."

However, this had not been the correct time to speak up. With speed that Kyle didn't realize John possessed, John thrust the knife towards Klaus. He had been holding the knife backhanded, and therefore didn't even need to change his grip. The knife plunged into Klaus's side. Somewhere between the 5th and 6th rib. Having been around violence for a rather long time, John knew this wouldn't immediately kill them man. It was very likely that his lung would collapse, however, as long as his blood clotted properly, he would survive long enough to speak. As the knife went into his Klaus's ribs, he made a guttural grunt, but didn't seem to be able to make any further sounds. John left the large blade firmly planted in Klaus's side and turned to Jack, not a single emotion playing across his face.

"Feel like talking yet?" The sentence came out as if he was simply discussing the weather. The question was so monotone and clear, it startled Kyle. That was the sign of a man who had nothing left to lose and had snapped. No sign of remorse, no sign of caring, just a deadpan look and a calm voice. This conveyed so much and so little at the same time.

"I — I do—- I don't know much." Jack said in the shaky voice of a man who was clearly shitting himself with fear. "I don't know where Gary took your son, I wasn't a part of that."

John reached out toward the knife, still sitting in Klaus's side. As he did this he didn't take his eyes off of Jack. Seeing this, Jack glanced at the knife and back to John. He continued, "B —- but, I know of one place that he has taken people like that to. He doesn't usually share the address of places that he takes people to, for this exact reason. Most of us only know one. He makes sure that somebody couldn't get the location of all of his safe houses from one person."

With a slight smile on his face, John said, "Well boy, where is this safe house."

"It— it's a large house off of North west 127th ave."

"Alright, you are going to point to it on a map and let me know where it is." As he said this John then looked over at Klaus. The knife was still sitting in his ribs, his breathing was shallow and he looked like he was losing consciousness. John reached over and pulled the knife out of his ribs. Of course, the rule of thumb if you want someone to stay alive, is to never pull out the object that is in the wound. When John pulled the knife out of Klaus's side, Klaus jolted upwards slightly, his eyes looked they would pop out of his skull. However, it didn't appear that Klaus had the ability to gasp. He tried, but ended up looking kind of like a fish out of water. It was evident what was happening, he was slowly drowning in his own blood. John knew he might live for another half hour without medical attention.

"Well Klaus, today is your lucky day, possessed help you call the ambulance, and they may just get here in time to save your life. But if you tell them who did this, I. WILL. HUNT. YOU. DOWN." John made sure to enunciate every word and syllable in the last 5 words. He wanted Klaus to fear him enough not to tell the police who did this. However, he knew it was unlikely that would happen even without the threat. John then told Gerand and Kyle to take the Challenger somewhere safe nearby to stash it. John then gave a smaller knife to Jack. "You look like you are healthy enough to leave, but I am sure if Klaus lives, he is going to keep that promise. You might think about your options here. He can't really fight back." He then took the handcuffs off the two men. By this time, Gerand was back with Kyle in tow. Gerand looked and them and waived, "Good luck gents, your going to need it." With that last moment Gerand drove off. John pulled the burner phone out of it's resting place inside of his pocket and dialed 911. He then tossed the phone to Jack, and they drove off on the motorcycles.

CHAPTER 10

John and Kyle both knew that it was not the best idea to ride the motorcycles, and that they needed to find another mode of transportation. They had strapped all of the guns to the backs of the hogs, but thought it best to find another vehicle. Since they couldn't drive either of their cars, they settled on stealing one. There were countless parking lots around Miami, and they knew that sooner or later there would be a cheap car they could easily break into. After about 10 minutes they pulled into the Northwest corner parking lot of the Westland Mall. They drove around a little looking at cars. The car they chose was a small 2 door Ford Escort. This was an older model and didn't appear to have any sort of alarm. Best of all, the car was a manual transmission. John had stolen many cars in his days of undercover work. The cars he liked to steal the most were manual transmission Fords. The older Fords, between 1990 and 1996 never had alarms unless they were high end models or after-market. John stopped the bike he was on and motioned to Kyle, "This one should do. Looks old enough." John got off the bike and rummaged through his bag on the back of the bike for a moment. He then produced a slim jim, and a plastic wedge. John was in a better mood at this point in time, and having pulled the tool out, he chuckled to himself. *Why name such an important tool a slim jim. Hard to take seriously.* John walked over to the Honda, simultaneously bending the end of the slim jim to the correct angle. It was such a simple tool, however, you had to know how to use one. He inserted the plastic wedge in between the window and the weather stripping, then he began to work. It didn't take him long, maybe 15 seconds to get the door unlocked. He opened the passenger door and reached over to unlock the driver side. Then he walked back over to the bike and grabbed a flat head screwdriver and a small hammer. Sitting in the driver seat of the car, he put the end of the screwdriver in the ignition and slammed it home a few times with the hammer. After jiggling the screwdriver and the ignition a bit, he was able to turn the screwdriver, and the car turned over. They then spend the next couple of minutes transferring everything to the trunk of the car. For how small these cars were, it always surprised John just how much room was in the trunk. This car making no exception in the impossibly large trunk category. The two men got in the car and got on the road. The drive was set to take about an extra 20 minutes from where they were.

As John drove along he thought about the events that had led him to where he was. He had never thought this sort of thing would ever happen to him. He always kept everything so compartmentalized. When he was undercover, he generally didn't even go home to see his family. This meant he had been away from home for a few months by the time this all happened. *Why me? Why did I have to seek the glory of taking down Frank. My family would all still be well and fine if I hadn't volunteered for this undercover role.* At this thought, John hit the top of the steering wheel with a fist. Kyle looked over at him, "How are you holding up?"

"Well Kyle, how do you think I am holding up. My wife is dead, my son has been kidnapped, and I am apparently also now a fugitive."

The statement unnerved Kyle but he pushed on. "Hey, I know that you are not okay in that regard. What I want to know is how your body is holding up. We have both been awake for over 24 hours. I want to make sure, if we go in guns blazing that I can count on you not to die." This statement seemed to calm John down slightly. "I am good enough. I have to be, sleep isn't going to help. It will just end in nightmares. And right now I don't feel like facing those nightmares."

"Fair enough, Why don't you stop at a gas station so we can get something to keep us on our toes."

A few minutes later John pulled into a gas station on the side of the road. The suggestion wasn't a bad one. And whoever owned this car didn't keep any gas in it. The two men got out of the car after parking next to a gas pump. John took a mental note of the gas pump number. *Pump 4.*

They walked into the gas station and John walked up to the man at the counter. He looked to be a young kid. Early 20's with long brown hair. *Kid looks like a damn girl.* John didn't say out loud. "Can I get 20 on pump 4?" Saying this John tossed a $20 bill on the counter.

"Uhh... sure." The kid said. His eyes were drifting to the gun on John's hip. John caught his gaze and gave him a firm look. The kid looked like he was about to shit himself. "I— I don't want any trouble." The kid said, stammering and trying to keep himself from crying. John could understand the kids confusion, he wasn't in a police uniform and didn't have his badge on his hip. However he always carried one. Pulling it out of his pocket he flashed it to the kid. "Calm down kid. I'm a detective. No need to go shitting yourself." This didn't seem to calm the poor boy down. "I— I know you're a detective. But — but."

"Spit it out boy!" John said in a rather harsh tone.

"The news has your face all over it. They are saying you are armed and dangerous."

"You hear that Kyle?"

Kyle had been in the back of the store gathering drinks and chips, but had just approached the counter. "Yeah, we better get the hell out of here." He paused. They still needed gas, and the snacks would keep them going. "Any chance you can let us fill up and get these snacks before you call the police? We aren't going to hurt you. We aren't robbers, we just want to pay and leave."

The kid looked at Kyle bewildered. "Yeah, I suppose you can still pay." He eyed Kyle sidelong. "But if I don't call it in, I'll get fired. I'll give you ten minutes to fill up and get out of here."

"Thanks kid," Kyle said. A moment later he pulled a crisp $100 bill out of his wallet and tossed it on the counter."Keep the change kid."

When they got out to the car, Kyle filled up the gas while John got into the car. After about 3 minutes, Kyle stopped pumping gas and put the cap back. He was about to get into the car when they heard sirens. "SHIT," said John, "We need to get out of here."

By the time he finished his statement Kyle was in the car. They drove out of the gas station and got back on the road, trying to act as normal as possible. They were driving for about 60 seconds when they saw cops coming up on them rather fast. John pulled the car over, hoping that the cops didn't know it was them, and didn't look very carefully.

The cop cars went flying by John and Kyle, probably moving at about 95 miles per hour. As the cars drove by, the little ford escort rocked back and forth from the air pressure around the police cruisers. John and Kyle waited there for roughly another minute or so. "Thank. God." Kyle said, making sure to pronounce every word. "Don't count your blessings yet. We don't know where they are going, or if any of them recognized us. Let's just keep going and pray that we weren't seen."

The rest of the 15 minute drive was peaceful. The police cruisers didn't come back the way they had gone, and when they turned onto the road that led to the house, neither of them saw anything out of the ordinary.

John drove by the property so both him and Kyle could get a good look at the layout. It was just after 2 am by the time they pulled up, so they couldn't see much. The most notable part of the house was that there were no exterior lights on. There were no guards outside, and just a few bikes parked out front.

John parked the car on the side of the road a few hundred yards down. There were lots of trees on either side of the residence, so that was going to be how they approached the house. They went over their plan a few times to finalize the details before they went in.

CHAPTER 11

As they scouted around the property looking for an entrance, they also took note of that fact that there did not appear to be any exterior cameras. Their plan to enter the building was a simple one. First Kyle ran over to the front of the house where the choppers sat, and proceeded to shove a couple. This would accomplish two things. The first of which was to make a loud raucous out front in order to draw out any interior guards. The second was to make sure that any survivors would not be able to leave quickly. As the choppers were rather large, they were not easy to stand back up after they had fallen over.

As the motorcycles fell over they made a fairly loud crashing sound. John noted that the bikes must have been even heavier than they thought, because they made a sound you would hear from 2 blocks. Kyle then ran around the side of the house and waited in the dark for phase 2 of their plan to come together. John was on the opposite side of the house. 2 men came outside with flashlights to inspect the noise. "Son of a Bitch," one exclaimed in a rather deep voice. He continued, "JACOB, I told you to make sure the bikes wouldn't fall over. You know how heavy these damn things are." The man with the deep voice appeared to be a husky man, about 5' 10" probably weighing in at 320 Lbs. The second man, obviously named Jacob, was a smaller guy, about 5'6" and looking somewhere in the neighborhood of 185 Lbs. "Get your ass over here and help me lift these damn bikes." The man with the deeper voice was snapping his fingers at Jacob, trying to get his attention. As they both started to lift one of the bikes, John and Kyle took that moment to pounce. They snuck up behind the two men rather quickly, and before either could think, they were both in a choke hold with the life being squeezed out of them. Since the bigger man was near Kyle, he had to deal with him. Neither man got a sound out at first. However, after about 10 seconds the larger man was beginning to break free. John squeezed harder and after about another 15 seconds, Jacob went limp. By this time however, the larger man managed to break free of Kyle's grip. Luckily, all of the squeezing from Kyle had left the man with a raspy throat unable to make much more than a wheezing sound. As he approached Kyle to attack, John ran up beside him and threw a right hook that would rival a horse's kick. Catching the man square in the temple, the punch was forceful enough that the man immediately lost consciousness, toppling onto his face and sliding a foot or two. As he had been moving sideways from John when the punch hit him, he continued to move that direction, just slightly away from John's fist.

Dragging the men to the side of the house where they wouldn't be seen, and proceeded to tie them up and gag the two so they would not be able to yell when they awoke. John and Kyle had both agreed that they did not wish to kill anyone they did not have to. After all, they were both cops, and killing people just for association felt wrong. When making their plans they agreed not to use deadly force unless someone decided to shoot at them. They were trying to be stealthy enough to not attract any unwanted attention. Before leaving the men, John grabbed the keys off of the larger man, thinking there was a chance they would be useful.

John and Kyle set off for the front door where the two men had come from, with any luck, no one would be immediately inside the door to spot them. Both men drew knives off their sides where they rested, just in case there was the need to use them. Approaching the front door, John could hear a TV on in the background, but it did not appear there were any lights on directly near the front door. John slowly pushed the door to open it a little more. When the two bikers had stepped outside, they hadn't closed the door completely. Slowly pushing the door inward, John and Kyle kept their eyes peeled for any danger. When the door was about half way open, John crept inside as slowly as he could, taking very deliberate steps to avoid making any noise. When John was almost through the door, he looked around, and not seeing anyone immediately, he motioned for Kyle to enter, bringing his index finger on his right hand and placing it against his lips, making sure Kyle knew to proceed with the utmost caution. After both men had entered the front door, they slowly closed it to the cracked position. They did not want to risk making any noise by latching it shut.

John and Kyle proceeded down the hallway towards the room the TV sound was coming from. Taking extra caution to check every corner. When they were about halfway down the hallway, John heard a man say to another, "I gotta take a piss. Better not unpause the show you prick."

They both took looked around frantically to figure out where the restroom was and where they could hide. The restroom ended up being right next to Kyle. Without a word, Kyle slipped into the bathroom to wait for the man. John looked around a little more and noticed a crawl space under the stairs that he was next to. Quickly he clambered into the crawl space trying not to make any noise. As he did so, his foot thumped against the wall. He quietly cursed himself and brought up his knife in case the man had heard him. However, instead of investigating the cause of the thump, the man just muttered, "friggin rats," and continued to the bathroom.

* * *

Inside the bathroom, Kyle took stock of his situation. The bathroom must have been more of a guest bathroom then anything else. It was rather small compared to the rest of the house. It had a standard standing shower with no tub, and a shower curtain. Directly across from the shower, was the toilet. And next to that was a sink. All in all the bathroom looked to be no bigger than about 7 foot squared.

Kyle slipped into the standing shower and waited for the man to enter the bathroom. He was just hoping that he wouldn't have to render the man unconscious as he was trying to take a shit. He heard the man mumble something about rats outside the door and come into the bathroom. He flicked on the lights and closed the door. As it turned out, the fan for this bathroom was powered by the same light switch and came to life. It was rather loud as well. The man walked over to the toilet and unzipped his pants. Right as he began to pee, Kyle put his hands together and looked up at the ceiling, thanking his good fortune. Kyle lunged out of the shower and within half a second had the man in a choke hold. Kyle squeezed so hard, and so immediately, that he was pretty sure he collapsed the man's windpipe from sheer force. The man tried to yell, but it came out as little more than a gasping, choking sound. The man tried to flail but do to Kyle's speed, he had him in a hold and on his knees before the man even had a thought to stop pissing. After about 45 seconds the man went limp, informing Kyle that he was out cold. Kyle stopped to look at the man and realized that he had pissed all over the place, including himself. With the noise of the fan, and his quick reaction speed, Kyle had managed to keep the interaction rather quiet.

* * *

After seeing Kyle return from inside the bathroom, John crawled out of his hiding spot. Both men creeped forward towards the room that the other man still sat in. On the way, John couldn't help but chuckle to himself, he could see that the man still in the room had decided to continue watching the show without his comrade. This was the best case scenario, because it meant that the man would be focused on the TV, and most likely wouldn't hear their approach. As they quietly entered the room, John noticed the man sitting on a couch with his back towards John and Kyle. He decided to take the opportunity that was presented. John quickly took his belt off and walked up to the back of the couch. With blindingly fast speed, John threw the belt around the man's neck and pulled back and down. The man started to flail, but the way in which John had done this, meant the man had no leverage to move. It lifted his body off of the couch and pulled just his head and neck over the back of the couch. This brought the man's feet up far enough that only the tip of his toes were touching the ground. For somewhere around 40 seconds the man flailed and grasped at the belt around his neck. However, due the John's speed and strength, the man had no chance. Soon, he went limp and John released the belt and the man slid back down to the couch. John put his fingers on the man's neck and checked to make sure he still had a pulse. Done with too much force, what John had done, could easily kill someone, and it was a very thin line. There was still a pulse, although thready, and ragged breathing. He would most likely live, and that was all John cared about.

John and Kyle had counted 7 bikes out front, that meant there were most likely 3 other men in the house. Upon this realization, John heard Kyle mumble his name and heard the click of the hammer being drawn back on a pistol. John wheeled, drawing his gun at the same time, but when he turned around he noticed that one person had a gun to Kyle's head, and two others were aiming at him. Taking stock of the situation, he knew he wouldn't be able to kill all three before at least one of them fired. He decided he couldn't take the chance that the one able to fire would kill Kyle.

"Drop it asshole." One of the men exclaimed after he had turned on them. The one in the center holding on to Kyle seemed the be the one giving directions. Slowly John lowered his gun to the ground and slid it toward the men, then stood up slowly, hands in the air and palms forward. The man to the right of John moved forward and picked up the gun, then stepped up and cold cocked John with the but of the gun he had in his hand. Kyle watched as John crumpled to the floor, out cold.

CHAPTER 12

Kyle woke up bound to what felt like a wooden beam. Looking around, he couldn't see anything. The room he was in was pitch black, and it felt like he was sitting on concrete. His head hurt like hell. He figured that they must have hit him the same way they hit John. That made him think, *Where is John?* He looked around frantically, hoping to see John. He couldn't see anything, *Damn, it's so dark in here.* Deciding it couldn't hurt, Kyle yelled to see if he could get a response. "JOHN." He paused to hear a response. *Nothing.*

"JOHN YOU THERE?"

Still no response. He muttered a stream of curses, and continued to think. *I have to find a way out of here.* He felt the rope that restrained his hands. It was fairly thick. *What about the wood?* He tried to feel around with his arms, and noticed that the beam was square. That meant that with enough time he could widdle down the rope on the corner of the wood beam. With escape in mind he started on the rope.

As he was carefully sawing at the rope, Kyle heard some voices and footsteps above him. All of the information he currently had told him he was in a basement. He thought to himself if was most likely the basement of the house that he and John had entered. He then heard the creak of a door above him, and light began to shine down into the room, spearing Kyle's eyes and making him wince from the pain of the light mixed with his pounding migraine. With this light he took stock of his surroundings that had previously eluded him. The first thing he noticed was that he was indeed alone in the basement. Though it looked as if he was not the first person to have been held down here. Off to his right Kyle could see a table lined with different tools that looked like they might be used for torture. The concrete beneath him was covered in blood stains and other marks. Other than the table covered in tools, there wasn't much in the room. Off to his left there were more wooden beams and a metal chair that was bolted to the floor. *I wonder why they didn't put me in that thing?* A few moments after the door was opened he heard a man growl, "Get in there," and then he saw John come tumbling down the stairs. Luckily enough for John, there weren't a large number of stairs before the bottom and they were wooden. As John tumbled down the stairs Kyle looked to where the light was coming from, and realized, they were not under the house. He could only see the one set of stairs, and behind the door there was sky, and some trees. He noted that this must be some sort of concrete bunker, and the door had to be facing east. The sun was coming in right through the front door, and it looked like a morning sun. By the angle at which he could see the sun, he judged that is must be about 9 am. That would have to mean he had been out for about 5 hours. *They must've hit me hard.*

He looked over at John as he hit the floor, landing on his back. He saw that John was stripped of his shirt and had cuts and scrapes all over him.

The man that had thrown John inside the bunker came down inside and looked at Kyle. "Oh, sleeping beauty is awake." Walking over to Kyle and looking at him. "Now we can really have some fun."

"Untie me, and we can have some fun Mano a Mano." Kyle said this with as much crazy in his eyes as he could. With strain, Kyle also stood up to look at the man eye to eye. The man walked up to Kyle with a big shit eating grin on his face. "You know, I can respect an answer like that, my name is Karl, whats yours?"

"Kyle, I'd shake your hand, but it looks like you are too much of a pansy to untie me."

Karl broke out in a hitching laugh. "I love it when the people that are tied up threaten me. The only thing that does, is make the torture last longer. Well, don't worry princess, I will untie you from the beam soon. But only long enough to strap you in that comfy chair over there so we can have a real conversation." With that he walked over to John, who had just begun to sit up, and kicked in in the ribs, making him double over. Then he hauled him up and threw him against another beam, then proceeded to tie him to the beam. After he had completed tying John to the pole, he walked back to Kyle, looked him dead in the eye, and punched him right in the kidney. This made Kyle gasp, and Karl laugh. "Now don't go anywhere ladies, I'll be back in a few to have some more fun."

Kyle turned to John, "What the hell happened to you? You look like shit"

"Well," John turned to Kyle, pausing to spit out some blood. "They must have hit you a bit harder than they hit me."

"Why do you say that?"

"Because I woke up down here about 3 hours ago and started yelling. But you wouldn't wake up. Glad to see you were just out cold and not dead."

"Yeah, I am pretty sure I have a concussion. My head is pounding." Kyle said this sentence with a grimace."

"Well, anyway," John continued, "After yelling for a few minutes, our good friend Karl came down here to shut me up. He was surprised you had woken either, but had told me you still had vitals. Naturally I didn't believe him, but it seems he wasn't lying. Well he drug me upstairs about 6 am it seemed. Light was just starting to come through that forest outside. He drug me into the house, on the way I took the liberty of pacing how far away we are. I'd wager we are about 50 yards from the main house. I think this was originally some sort of bomb shelter."

"Yeah, I figured that out too," Kyle said.

"Yeah, well while inside the house they started the usual routine of torture to figure out what I wanted, how I figured out where this place was, all of that. It doesn't actually appear they know why we were here. That should play to our advantage."

"Oh, they didn't know why we came here? You would think that would be forefront in their mind." Kyle said this with a bit of confusion.

"That's what I thought as well, but they didn't ask me about that, and they had no idea who I am. I didn't decide to enlighten them either. The way I figure it, if they know who we are and why we are here, they will just kill us and be done with it. Instead they are going to drag it out and try to get as much information as possible, which will give us time to formulate a plan of escape."

"Good thinking," Kyle said, "I was working on these ropes, the beams seem to have pretty crisp edges."

"That's not a bad plan," John said, smirking. "However, it appears these guys weren't really trained on searching someone. I still have the knife in my boot."

"Well you could've led with that asshole." Kyle said with a bit of sarcasm.

"I could've, but what would be the fun in that." John brought his right boot up to his hands and was quickly free of his ropes. He then walked over to Kyle and cut his ropes also.

"I want to wait until Karl comes back to escape. I think we can get some info out of him before we take off."

Kyle looked at John for a moment. "That doesn't seem smart, what if he brings people with him?"

John grinned again, "The dumbass cleared the house. When he came and got me he was alone, and there was only one other person in the house. When people are torturing a guy, you can bet everyone in the house is going to come watch. But it was just the two of them. They didn't realize they were giving me far more information than they were getting."

The two men formulated a plan and waited for Karl to return. This took a bit longer than they anticipated. From their perspective, it appeared to take about 45 minutes from when he left. Soon enough however, they heard the sounds of him unlocking the door and they both sat back down against the beams with their hands clasped behind their backs. John was holding onto his knife in case their plan went sideways. As Karl walked in, the sunlight in that background confirmed their timeline. It was now nearly 10 am and the sun was shining bright. Everything about this look made John chuckle to himself, Karl looked like a god descending to earth. The sun's bright light encircled him, washing out everything else they could see. It almost created a halo of light. Had it been better times, this would be awe inspiring, it really was a beautiful sight.

"Hello Ladies, I hope you have behaved yourselves nicely." Karl said this with a smirk on his face. He had flicked on an interior light and shut the door, so the holy image that was before them, no longer held. He descended the stairs lazily as if to suggest he was already bored by the situation. "What, no longer feeling chatty?" He said when neither of the men had bothered to respond to his first comment.

Karl immediately aimed for Kyle and walked over to him. "Hello Sunshine, let's get you in that comfy chair over there and get started shall we?" He motioned with his head toward the chair that was bolted the floor. "This is going to be fun."

"That sir, is finally something we agree on." Kyle said suddenly, with a smirk on his face. While Karl was stunned by Kyle's comment, he thrust hit foot upward towards Karl's abdomen. The kick connected with Karl's body and sent him stumbling backwards. Kyle could see that this move had instantly angered Karl. He reached into his waistband to pull out a gun, but by the time he had, John was already behind him. John yelled "HEY!," making Karl turn toward him momentarily, but this was all the time John needed. He was already in the air. John jumped in the air, turning his body to accelerate his kick and connected the top of his foot with the left side of Karl's head. This was a kick that had enough force immediately knock Karl unconscious, and sent his body back about 5 feet.

Kyle hurried over to check Karl and make sure the kick hadn't killed him. He still had a strong pulse, but there was blood pouring out of his head. "Shit John, you practically killed the man with that kick." Kyle said this with a bit of laughter.

"Well, hell, how was I supposed to know he couldn't take a kick." John said chuckling.

The two men stopped the bleeding and strapped Karl into the chair that he seemed to love so much. Looking around for something to wake him up with, John noticed a sink with a bucket. He went over and filled the bucket with water. *This water must come from an aquifer, it's rather cold.* John took the bucket of water over to Karl and threw the water in his face. The water splashed all over Karl soaking him. However, the water did the trick, and Karl woke up, rather unhappy. Karl looked around, momentarily confused by his situation, then it all came back to him.

"I'm guessing this in not how you thought your day was going to go, huh?" John asked sarcastically.

"What do you want?" Karl said, Letting his German accent fall, and speaking with a clear voice that didn't sound like it had any accent. *Was his German accent fake?* John thought, staring at Karl.

"Was the German accent fake?" John asked, confused.

"Yes," Karl said, "I have been working on Infiltrating Derr Hass for 3 years."

"Wait, who the hell are you?" Kyle interjected.

"I'm just from a rival gang. We want Derr Hass out of Florida. So I have been working on tearing them apart from the inside."

"Do you know who I am?" John asked. Pointing the end of his knife at Karl.

"Yes, but I am the only one that was in the house that knows who you are, and what you want. The others just thought you were from a rival gang."

Getting more agitated by the second John asked, "Where is he?"

"Look, Detective, I will lead you to your boy, but I need assurance you won't kill me. I very much enjoy living." Karl said this with a hint of fear in his voice.

"How about I just carve the information out of you?" John said with a snarl.

Karl looked at John with fear in his eyes, "I... I am the only one here who knows where your boy is, and I won't tell you if you torture me. The only way you get the information is if you let me live."

John lunged forward at Karl and put the knife to his throat, but all the guy did was flinch and close his eyes tightly. The fact that Karl was so obviously afraid of him, calmed him slightly.

"Why torture me if you knew who I was?"

"I had to show the guys in the house that I was with them, and I was hoping that you would be able to keep your mouth shut. We have orders to kill on sight. But almost no one knows what you look like."

John thought about this for a moment, and decided he could buy that. "Alright fine, one last question. How do you know who I am?"

At this Karl looked a little scared, "I .. I.." He paused again.

This agitated John, and so he stepped up to Karl and put the knife against his throat and yelled, "TELL ME!"

Looking more scared than ever, Karl said, "I was with Neitz when he went to your house. I saw some pictures of you. But there were only three of us; Neitz, his right hand Jackal, and myself. I tried to keep them from killing your wife, but Frank gave specific instructions, and Neitz was much more afraid of Frank than of any backlash from you."

John was shaking with anger. Screaming, he asked, "DID YOU TOUCH MY WIFE?"

Right about then, Kyle intervened, knowing they needed Karl. He rushed up and pulled back John still shaking with anger.

"NO... No, I just stood watch." Karl said, his voice faltering from fear.

Kyle then spoke up, "John, we need him alive, you need to calm down. Please, DO.. NOT... KILL... HIM." Kyle said this last bit with as much empathy as he could muster. He wanted to kill Karl as well, but could see that they needed him alive much more than dead.

"John, I know this hurts, but please, he can lead us to Lane. Please try to see that. He was just there to stand watch. He didn't do anything."

John was starting to calm down, but still looked like he wanted to beat Karl til his skull caved in. John took a few deep breaths, and managed to get his anger under control. "Alright, I won't kill him," John paused for a moment to stare at Karl, "YET." He said this with emphasis. John stared Karl in the face, then finally asked, "Is your name actually Karl?"

CHAPTER 13

John and Kyle spent the next 20 minutes questioning Karl on everything. It turned out his name actually was Karl, which made things a lot easier and less confusing.

"Look, I know where all of the warehouses and and buildings owned by *Der Hass* are, but I do not know which one they are holding your son in." Karl said defensively.

John glared at him, "I thought you said you knew where he was?"

Karl looked back at John, deadpan, "Was, I knew where he was, but knowing Neitz, he is going to move him every 24 hours or so. The man is paranoid. Obsessive even. So he doesn't like to stay in the same place for more than 24 hours. But if we go where I know he was, we might be able to get some information."

"Well then that is where we will start." John said, "You got a car?"

Karl looked hesitant, but reluctantly he said, "Yeah, it's in the front yard, but I have to come up with a good enough reason to drive it back here."

Kyle piped up then, "Just tell them we didn't know anything so you killed us and you want to get rid of the bodies." Kyle paused for a moment. "When you drive it back here, you can put us in the trunk until we are clear of the property and you can let us out."

John thought about it for a moment, "I don't like it, how can we be sure he will let us out of the trunk?"

Karl chuckled momentarily, "Dude, all trunks have interior latches these days, can't get rid of em either."

"Good point, go get the car." With this last sentence, John shoved Karl in the direction of the door. Karl growled slightly but then moved toward the door. When he had left, Kyle spoke up again. "Dude, I know you are angry, but you have to cool it."

"I'll cool it when I get my son back. He may not have done the deed, but he was there. The only reason he isn't dead is because we need him." John said with a growl.

"What was he supposed to do?" Kyle said, throwing up his hands. "Tell the leader of the gang, that he didn't want to participate. No, you know better than anyone, turning down those types of things makes you look suspicious and weak. He needed to maintain his cover."

"I don't give a shit. He said he is from a rival gang. Which means he is just as guilty as everyone else." John said, raising his voice.

Kyle conceded, "I guess you have a point, but try not to provoke him too much before we find Lane. He is no good to us dead, and if you push him around enough, one of you will wind up dead."

"Alright, fine. But I still don't trust the bastard." John said.

* * *

10 minutes later, Karl opened the door to the bunker. "Come on, quickly, get in the trunk." Karl said, waving his hands frantically. "What's the hurry?" John said.

"The guys in the house said they wanted to help load you up. I said no, now they are coming. Just get in the trunk and act dead." Karl said frantically. The two men begrudgingly complied, and got in the trunk quickly. When they got in and had turned their faces to look at the seats, Karl shut the trunk. A moment later John and Kyle heard a man say something to Karl. "Hey, we said we would help you."

John could hear Karl pretending to pant, "That's alright guys, I wanted to do it this time."

"Can we see them before you take off with em?"

There was a pause, "I guess so, but make it quick, I have other things I need to do today." Karl said, sounding annoyed. Both men took a large breath and held it, keeping as still as possible. Karl popped the trunk and some people looked inside. "They don't look all that beat up, how did you kill them?" One man asked.

"After the first wouldn't talk I just decided to kill both of them. And I gave them both an embolism. Hard to trace, and works rather well when injected in the right spot."

"What the hell is an embolism?" One of the men asked.

Karl responded by shutting the trunk, letting the two men breathe again. "You inject an air bubble into the bloodstream. If you do it properly, they have a heart attack and die." He said exasperatingly. "Don't worry yourselves about it, there is a reason I am the one that takes care of these things."

"Huh, interesting, alright then." John heard one of the guys say, and then heard them walk off. Then the car started up and the started traveling. After about 5 minutes, the car stopped and Karl came around and opened the trunk. "Smart move, convincing them of an embolism." Kyle said as he climbed out of the trunk. "How did you think up that one so quick."

"They aren't the brightest bulbs in the box. I saw it on a TV show once. Figured they would buy it, or at least they would need time to figure out I was lying." Karl said with a shrug. "Neitz likes the kind that don't generally think for themselves. Ones that just follow directions without questions."

"Well either way, nice cover." Kyle said as John was crawling out of the trunk.

"We need to go back to the car for the guns." John said matter of factly.

"That won't work," Karl said, "After your initial attack we canvassed the neighborhood and found the car that you had parked down the road. The guns are in the house, and we are not going to be able to get back in."

"Great," John said, "Well then take us to the Wharf's storage container yard." He said this last bit motioning for Karl and Kyle to get back in the car."

As they drove, Kyle and Karl chatted, and John brooded in the back seat.

"So, you said you are from a rival gang? What gang would that be?" Kyle asked.

"Not one that you have likely heard of. We like to work behind the scenes. Unlike other gangs that like to make their presence known, we prefer to be behind the curtain. We believe that being a known gang makes you a target, for both law enforcement, and other gangs. The name the Gang goes by is *Die Vorhang.*"

That caught John's attention. John quickly drew his knife and lunged forward. Holding the knife to Karl's throat. "I thought you said that you weren't part of *Der Hass?*" John said, seething.

"I am not a part of that Gang. I am a part of *Die Vorhang.* And I said rival gang, did I not. Our founders are of German Heritage." Karl said rather calmly for a man driving a car with a knife on his throat.

"John," Kyle said, locking eyes with him, "Let go of him. We need him alive." Kyle said this last bit as sternly as he could manage.

John grumbled, "Fine," and sat back in the seat behind Karl.

"As I was saying," Karl began, "The gang is of German descent. *Der Hass* knows about us, but believes that we only operate in Germany. However, most of our member base is here in Florida. We have many members that operate from within *Der Hass.* But that is the way we work, and why we are so successful at staying in the shadows. We do not operate normally. We operate as a covert government agency might, from within other organizations. We decided about 4 years ago that *Der Hass* needed to be dismantled here.We do not condone the types of acts this gang has committed and they have also taken much of our business. Just as any other gang does, our funding comes from drugs. However, we operate without much in the way of casualties."

"How do you run a gang without killing people?" Kyle asked, honestly interested in the topic.

"Persuasion." Karl said, nonchalantly.

"What kind of persuasion?" Kyle asked.

"Well mostly we pay people off to leave us alone. Some we threaten, and very few we have to kill. Usually people listen to reason when you come in with a mixture of money and threats."

"I see, that is why *Der Hass* needs to go, right? They are cutting into your ability to quiet people with money." Kyle said, putting together the pieces.

"Exactly." Karl said. "We have been working to tear apart this group from the inside. However, it is proving difficult. They have a strong grasp on Miami. But if you make enough noise, and get rid of enough people, well, it will help us immensely."

"I see," Said Kyle, " That is why you are helping us. You are hoping we destabilize the gang enough for your people to complete your job."

"Correct, but more so, I detest everything Neitz has done to John's family. In order to stay in cover I had to be there, but I can't stand treating women and children like that. Our group may cast threats upon families, and occasionally we have to kidnap to get our point across, but we would never, ever, go so far as to murder a wife and take a son. Our organization does not condone such actions." Karl said with feeling. "I want Neitz to be taken out, for the sole purpose of ridding the earth of his evil."

"At least we agree on one thing." John commented.

The rest of the ride was fairly silent, and they arrived at the Wharf a few minutes later. As they were pulling up, they instantly regretted their choice to return to the Wharf.

CHAPTER 14

The entire Wharf was swimming with cops. As they approached, they saw flashing lights and people running around. Karl stopped the car and started backing up. It appeared they were able to go unnoticed, due to how far away they were from the Wharf. Karl drove to a high spot and they all got out of the car to investigate. "Shit," John said, pointing at something. "They found the container. Looks like we aren't going back there."

"Yeah, there is no way we are getting in there unnoticed, and it looks like they already locked up all the guns anyway. Must be a hundred officers down there." Kyle remarked.

John was rubbing his chin and staring at Karl, "Yeah..." He said. " Karl, do you know someone that we can get guns from?"

Karl paused for a moment, seeming to ponder the idea. "Yeah, I know a place, but it isn't going to be cheap. Do you have money somewhere?"

Due to his line of work, John always prepared for this type of situation. He had stashes all over Miami, just like in the shipping container. However, Kyle did not know about them. " Yeah, I have a couple of places." John said looking to Kyle for his reaction to this news.

"Wait, you have more stashes than the ones I know about?" Kyle asked.

"Yeah," John said, "I like to be prepared, and I —"

Kyle cut him off, "I understand, I just didn't think you were that practical. I figured you told me about all of your stashes. Glad you didn't."

John thought about all of his stashes, trying to figure out which one was closest. They all usually had cash, an Identity, and a pistol. He thought about his cousins house over in Hialeah, but figured the PD would be monitoring all of his family for contact. His next best option was the Indian Creek Country Club. He had a permanent locker at the club under one of his aliases. He hoped that with all of the aliases he had, the PD wouldn't have had time to get to the Club. John spoke up then, "Karl, you know where the Indian Creek Country Club is?"

Karl thought for a moment, "Is that the one that is north of Normandy Shores, about half an hour north east?"

"Yeah, West on 91st off of the A1A." John said.

"Yeah I know where that is, let's go before anyone notices us here." Karl said quickly.

They all agreed and got in the car. A couple of minutes into the ride, John passed out. He was still extremely tired, and needed a few minutes of shuteye.

* * *

"John," Kari said, "John, help me." John looked around frantically, trying to find the source of the voice he was hearing. "I can't see you." John said with feeling. He was in a pitch black room. He couldn't see anything. He felt the ground and noted that it felt like carpet. Still frantic he began to crawl around, trying to find the direction of Kari's voice. But the voice seemed to be coming from every direction at once, still calling out. "John, help me.. John, please." By now John was in tears, frantic from the voice. Then he heard a new voice come in from all around him. "Daddy.." John instantly knew who the voice belonged to. "Lane, Daddy is here, where are you buddy?" Still frantic John reached what felt like a wall. He reached up and found a light switch. Flipping the switch, he saw a faint glow off to his left. There he saw Kari, sitting in a chair with her wrists tied down. He saw Lane sitting in his own chair, hands bound. Then he saw a shadow lumber into view behind Kari. The face he saw angered him. It was Frank. Frank stood behind Kari with a knife in his hand. The man was wearing an evil grin, the kind only a madman would. John started to run towards them. He heard Kari pleading, "John, please

hurry,.. John, please." Frank lifted the knife slowly. Slower than he should have and rested it against Kari's neck. John was still running, but despite how fast he pumped his legs, he couldn't move fast enough. He didn't seem to be gaining ground. He called out, "NO, DON'T DO IT FRANK. DON'T DO IT." But the evil grin on Franks face remained steady. "Oh my dear boy it's already done." He heard Frank say. Still running toward the two, John couldn't reach them. Then Frank drew the knife across Kari's neck in a deliberate motion.

John startled awake, breathing heavily, with tears streaming down his face. Based on the fact that the car was still moving he wagered that he hadn't been asleep for very long. Kyle looked back at John, hearing him rustle in the backseat. "Another nightmare?" Kyle asked.

John wiped the tears from his face and sat up. "Yeah, I can't seem to get any shuteye without one invading my mind."

"Well shake it off. We are almost there." Kyle said. "What alias did you use here anyway?"

"This one is Gerald Hyland." John said.

Kyle thought for a moment. "Gerald Hyland, wasn't that the one you used to take down that human trafficking ring like 5 years ago?"

"That's the one." John said, "Saved about 50 girls from being sold."

* * *

Karl pulled up to the country club and John got out. Kyle and Karl were going to wait in the car. John figured it would draw less attention if he went in alone.

"Good Day Mr. Hyland." The butler said, "We weren't expecting you, otherwise we would have had your room ready."

"Unnecessary Robert, I'm not staying. I've simply come to get some items out of my storage downstairs." John said. "Could you open the door to the basement for me?"

"Of course Mr.Hyland," Robert said, "Will there be anything else that I can assist you with?"

"No that will be fine." John said back. "Thank you!"

The two men walked toward the door in the country club that led downstairs. Only certain members even knew about the existence of this room. It was there for people to leave items, if they had enough money to purchase the space. Naturally the police department had sanctioned the purchase, but because the purchase was a lifetime guarantee, the space never expired, and was available 24/7. As they stopped at the door, Robert turned to him "You look remarkably like a man that is on the run right now. Some detective named John."

John stopped and eyed Robert, "You must be talking about John Mauser. He's a cousin of mine. My family all looks alike, specially the guys. It's uncanny really."

Robert paused a moment longer, "Well not my business anyway, hope he is alright." Then he unlocked the door and let John in.

John stepped toward the familiar staircase. This was an unusual staircase, the steps were large, probably 2 feet wide, and the staircase descended at a leisurely pace. The corridor he was in was lit by a row of dim lights along the wall that rounded with the staircase. The walls were painted red, leaving a reddish glow to the room. The mixture of items along with the curving staircase, gave this corridor an ominous tone. John had often been slightly put off by the staircase, but it only looked like it did out of strange coincidence. Also, due to the fact that the staircase went underground, it was completely concrete, which echoed every step. As John descended downward, he could hear nothing but his own steps. Along with the PD he was able to shut down the ring of human traffickers, but they had not managed to gather enough evidence to shut down the country club, and therefore, this staircase, that led down to where many criminals kept their items, remained.

When he reached the room that housed all of the storage units, he looked around and noticed that it looked as though the room had not been touched in over a year. Only a select few had keys to the room, and none of the staff was allowed past the door, even for emergencies. There was only one person who was allowed in the room, and that was the creator. The room was roughly the size of small apartment. Probably one thousand square feet in total. Each wall was lined with storage units, roughly the size of a standard cubicle. They were only roughly 4 feet wide, but were about 5 feet deep. They were not meant to house large amounts of items, and although being called storage units, they were more like closets. The room resembled a room of doors, each one leading into one unit. The doors were heavy steel doors, painted red, with fingerprint scanners attached to the handles. The fingerprint scanner also had two backup systems, a heartbeat monitor read your heartbeat through your thumb. This verified that the thumb was attached to a body that was still alive. Then there was a voice analyzer that you had to speak a phase into. If either one of these items did not match, then the unit would be locked for one hour.

John found the unit he needed, unit 37, and walked over to it. He wiped off the scanner and held his thumb to it. You had to hold your thumb in place for about 15 seconds, while it scanned your fingerprint and read your heart rate. The machine blinked green and beeped one solid tone. Then John spoke, " E pluribus unum. Et ex una, multi."

John heard a ding, and a small light in the center of the door turned green. He heard the mechanism unlatch, and he pulled the door open. Inside the room, were the exact items he had left there. There were a couple of suits hanging on one side of the room. On the other side there was a rack. The rack was about 4 feet off of the ground. On it rested, a large amount of cash. Probably twenty thousand dollars, a passport, and a handgun. Of course the handgun was a 1911, chambered in .45 ACP. The passport belonged to Gerald Hyland, and had a matching drivers license tucked inside. Hanging with the clothes was also a thin bullet proof vest. One that was meant to be worn under other clothes without being noticeable. John decided to slip into one of the suits he had hung there. Taking care to fasten the bullet proof vest between the undershirt and dress shirt. On the floor was a small bag that he stuffed the cash into, then he put the gun in his waistband.

In order to be secure, the unit had to be locked from outside in a similar fashion. You had to close the unlocked door, and speak a lock phrase aloud. In order to quell confusion, everyone had the same lock code. John stepped out of the room and pushed the door closed, then he said, "Lock." The door chimed and the fingerprint scanner lit up, he then held his thumb on the scanner for roughly 5 seconds. He heard a second chime, and the light on the door flashed red, and he heard the mechanism engage. John walked up the stairs toward the lobby. When he got to the door, he rang a doorbell and within 30 seconds, Robert returned and opened the door. "Will that conclude your business for today, Mr. Hyland?" Robert asked. "Yes, thank you very much Robert." John said, and handed the man a twenty dollar bill. "Thank you for your generosity sir." Robert said and walked John to the front door. When John spotted the car in the parking lot he strode over and hopped in the backseat.

"Everything go alright?" Kyle asked.

"Without a hitch," John said, "But I recommend we leave soon. I don't trust these people and I am pretty sure they called in an anonymous tip."

"Off we go then." Karl said and started up the car.

CHAPTER 15

As the three men pulled onto A1A North, they saw lights from police cars approaching in both directions. Karl pulled the car onto the freeway and drove at a normal pace, making sure not to draw too much attention to the vehicle.

"So what kind of guns does this guy have?" John asked.

"Just about anything you need," Karl said casually. Continuing he said, "He has rifles, shotguns, pistols, hell, I've even seen a crossbow."

"Interesting." John said. "How far away is he?

"He is about 40 minutes Northeast. Over by the North Perry Airport." Karl said.

"Really," John said, "Your gun dealer lives near an airport, and hasn't been busted yet?"

"It works for him, considering he uses it to smuggle most of the weapons. He is a private pilot. And he uses his airplane a lot. Only a portion of the time is used to smuggle. He is a pretty careful guy." Karl said.

"Well, if he is as careful as you say he is, what makes you think he is going to sell to some detectives on the run from the Law?" Kyle asked.

"Well, possibly because I am vouching for you." Karl said, looking at Kyle quickly.

"Why does your vouching for us carry so much weight?" John asked.

Karl looked into the rear view mirror for a moment and cautiously answered, "Because he is my brother, and because he generally does what I want. I was the one that helped him start up his little industry. I funded it. He doesn't generally ask questions when I bring someone to him."

"Well that's handy." Kyle said.

"Sure is, he has always looked up to me. But the last year or two he has really taken off. He runs everything himself. I am the only one that knows his true identity. He goes by "The Seller." Karl said nonchalantly.

"Holy shit, I know him, we have been trying to nail him forever. But we could never figure out who he was, and he keeps everything so compartmentalized. It is really impressive." Kyle said.

"Yeah, maybe don't tell him that part." Karl said.

"Agreed." John piped up from the back of the car.

* * *

As they pulled into the driveway, they could see that he really was doing well for himself. His house was a 3 story mansion. It had a private gate blocking the driveway, that had a keypad for entrance. The gates themselves, surrounding the property had to be 15 feet tall. They were made out of what appeared to by ½ inch steel beams. His property had to span 2 acres in total, and the house and garage took up most of that room. The house was an Italian design, it had a huge archway leading to the front door, and massive windows over the front of the house. The driveway was a circular courtyard of red and white brick designs. With a massive water fountain in the center. The water fountain had Poseidon holding a Trident above his head in one hand, and a rifle in the other pointed forward. Water appeared to swirl up Poseidon's arm and fan out over the Trident. As well as the water that came out of the end of the gun. The exterior of the house was white in color, with green plants and vines growing on it in a purposeful fashion.

As they pulled in a man came out of the front door, with a pistol in his right hand, and a stern look on his face. The man was roughly 5'11" and appeared to weigh in the neighborhood of 190 lbs. He looked very fit, but had a similar facial structure to Karl. He was wearing a 3 piece suit Grey suit that was likely a custom fit. He had hair that was a bit long, but that was slicked back in a fashion that made him look younger than he was. He wore a serious look on his face that said he did not take unannounced visitors lightly. He looked over at Karl with a snarl, "You brought detectives to my house, Brat." When he spoke, there was a heavy Russian accent to his words.

"Dasvidaniya, Brat." Karl remarked. "Why don't you invite us inside. There are many ways to see a man outside."

"Why are there detective in my front yard?" The man questioned. "Let alone detectives that are currently on the run."

Karl grinned slightly, "That is the reason exactly, they mean to do business, not to investigate or arrest." Karl motioned for John to open the duffel bag he had in his hands. John reached down and opened the zipper slightly, revealing the cash inside the bag.

"Well, why didn't you say so in the first place. Come in, come in, as Karl said, there are many ways to see a man outdoors." The man said, and slipped the pistol back into his waistband.

As they walked inside the house, it was easy to tell this man obviously made good money selling weapons. The house was just as lavish on the inside as the property was on the outside. Looking around, John could see that this man had a taste for the fancy. In the foyer there was a grand piano that was shined to a black finish with what appeared to be specks of gold in the paint. The foyer itself was large enough to fit 50 or 60 people, and was marble and glass. Walking through the entryway, they went underneath the stair and entered what appeared to be a personal library. The room was large, probably 600 square feet, and was lined with bookshelves. The carpet in the room was was you would expect to find in a library. An auburn red carpet that was short and kept clean. Every shelf was covered in books, and there was even a ladder attached to the shelves in order to get the books that were high off the ground. John watched as "The Seller" walked up to one of the bookshelves and put his thumb on what appeared to be the spine of a book. Shortly afterwards, a doorway slid open just in front of the man, revealing a well lit staircase. "The Seller" waived for them to enter the stairwell.

The stairwell descended downwards for what appeared to be 3 stories. Entering the room below, John noticed that the area was about as large as the building upstairs. The walls were lined with every gun he could think of. There were even some guns that John didn't think would be possible to get into the United States. There was an island station covered in different types of grenades. It appeared that he even had RPG's, and a couple of SMAW's.

"I'm impressed," John started, "Where did you manage to get a SMAW?'

"A magician never reveals his secrets." The Seller said in a condescending tone. "Plus, I am already selling to two detectives, which is the stupidest thing I have done all year. Why would I tell you how I get my gear?"

"Fair point." John said.

"Now, did I let you come down here just to admire my collection, or are you interested in buying anything. If you aren't buying you need to get out of my house." The seller said.

"Alright, alright," John said, "We need two assault rifles, M4 preferably equipped with 4-X sights and canted Irons. We need two handguns, I prefer the 1911, but I will take any .45 with tritium sites. I expect we need at least a thousand rounds of 5.56. About 200 rounds of .45, and whatever pistol and ammo he needs." As John said this he jerked his thumb towards Kyle.

The Seller gave him an amused look, "So nothing too specific then huh?"

John gave The Seller a dry look, "If you don't have what we need we will find someone who does."

"Woah, woah, woah, I was just poking fun man." The Seller backtracked. "I have everything you need and more." Looking at Kyle he said, "Now what kind of pistol do you fancy?"

Kyle seemed to ponder the question for a moment, "I'll take a .45, same as him." Kyle said, pointing to John.

"Wonderful," the seller said, " Give me just a moment to put everything together for you and you can be on your way," With that The Seller started hustling around the room grabbing everything that was requested. By the time he was done, two M4's lay on the table with 10 mag's of ammo and about 3 extra boxes. One 1911 with tritium sights and 4 mag's lay next to it. A glock with similar sights lay next to that with a similar number of magazines. And a box of 200 rounds sat next to that.

"Check to make sure everything works as advertised, and then we can talk price." The Seller said.

John and Kyle both picked up the Handguns, racked the slides and made sure the sights were working before slipping them into their own waistbands. Then they picked up the M4's and racked the bolts to make sure they cycled correctly.

"Looks good to me," John said, "I'll give you twelve large for everything."

The seller chuckled, " Is that a joke? The M4's alone are Fifteen. I need at least eighteen for everything."

John looked around the room pondering the price. "I'll give you Sixteen and you throw in two of those level 5 vests."

The seller chuckled again, "You drive a hard bargain for a man in your position. How about Seventeen with the vests."

"Alright, you've got a deal." John said, and put the bag on the table with the money and took out four stacks of money. He threw three on the table and separated part of the fourth stack and set it down next to the other three. "You can count it if you want, but it's all there." John said, picking up one of the M4's and slinging it across his back. As John packed up the ammo in the bag, The Seller quickly fanned the cash in his fingers, doing a cursory count. Kyle picked up his rifle as well slinging it across his back.

As they were approaching the stairs a light started flashing and a quiet alarm went off. John heard the Seller quietly curse to himself. He turned around with fire in his eyes, "Did you set me up?"Looking at Karl accusingly.

"I would never, you know that." Karl said, with a little hurt in his voice.

"Well someone did, otherwise the cops wouldn't be at my gate trying to get it." The Seller said angrily.

John put up his hands, "Look they probably had a Bolo out on the plate, but they can be easily dissuaded. The two of you should go up there and let them know that there is no one else here. They are looking for the two of us, just tell them there must have been a mistake on the plate."

The Seller thought it over for a second or two. "That's a good plan." Then he looked at Karl, "Let's go say hello to our guests. As for you two, there is a monitor over there where you can see what is going on outside.

As The Seller and Karl ascended the stairs John and Kyle went to the monitor that displayed the front yard. There were also speakers with which to use. The two men watched as The Seller and Karl approached the officers outside.

As he approached the gate, The Seller held his arms wide in a T shape. "Is there something I can do for you today officers?" He said.

One of the officers spoke in a commanding voice, "Open this gate, we have reason to believe that you are harboring fugitives."

"And what reason would that be?" The Seller asked.

"That BMW parked in your yard was spotted leaving the scene of a crime earlier today. The fact that it is parked in your driveway suggests you may be harboring fugitives." The same officer answered.

Karl spoke up then, "Look officers, this is my car, and I just came to visit my cousin. However, I can assure you that this car did not leave the scene of any crimes. Do you perhaps have the wrong BMW? There are a lot in this city."

A second officer then spoke up," If you don't open this of your own accord, we will have no choice but to break it down."

The Seller chuckled, "While I would applaud your ability to get the gate open, you would receive a hefty lawsuit for damages. However, I have nothing to hide, you are more than welcome to step inside the gate." As he spoke The Seller waved at a an standing in the gate control room. The gate swung open and the officers walked inside. "Look officers, there is no one here, save for my staff, my woman, and the two of us. Please inspect the car if you must, but please be swift, I have a meeting I must return to soon."

The officers searched the car, and found nothing. The lead officer came near and spoke to The Seller. "We haven't found anything, but if I find out you are lying, I will come back with whatever means necessary to open your gate and get inside."

The Seller grinned, "Like I said officer, I would applaud your ability to get that gate open. Now have a nice day." With that he turned on his heels and walked towards the house.

The officer paused for a moment, then knowing he had no recourse for action decided to walk away.

When The Seller and Karl returned to the basement, The Seller looked at John and Kyle, "You will need to take the secondary exit and find your own ride. Karl's car is burnt and the cops will be watching for some time."

"There is a second exit?" Kyle asked, slightly surprised.

"Of course. When you are in my industry, you never leave only one exit. It is right over there, behind the rack of vests." The Seller pointed over to where the vests hung on the wall. After pointing he walked over, and pressed a hidden button next to one of the vests. With that, the wall swung inwards, revealing a long corridor.

"Where does it exit?" John asked.

"Two hundred yards down, the tunnel will T. You will want to go to the right. To the left comes up in a building at the airport, to the right will take you about half a mile away and comes up into a small house. The cops shouldn't be looking over there. But you will need to get a ride quick. Six houses to the North of the house is a neighbor that is always gone. You should be able to steal one of his cars without too much hassle." With that bit of information The Seller held out his hand and offered it to John. John clasped his hand and said, "Thank you for your help."

The Seller smirked, "Don't mention it, and please, forget who I am."

John nodded, and the three men started jogging down the path.

CHAPTER 16

Coming to the end of the path and entering the residence the three men took stock of the situation.

"Look," Karl began, "I can't really continue this with you. I need to get back to my car and leave my cousins residence. However, I can tell you about the places that Frank is likely holding your son."

"Well you better start talking," John said. "Because we don't have a lot of time."

"Alright, well, there are 3 likely places to begin. There is a large warehouse that doubles as a chop shop for Frank. That is the most likely. The others are different types of storage facilities." Karl said.

Over the next few minutes, Karl told them of all of the places and where they were located.

"So you are sure he is in one of these places. Would you bet your life on it?" John asked casually.

'Look," Karl said, "If he isn't in one of these places, Frank took him somewhere that no one knows about."

"Alright," John said in a tense tone, "Thank you for your help."

"Not a problem," Karl said, turning to walk towards the entrance to the tunnel.

After waiting for Karl to leave, John looked towards Kyle, determination in his eyes. "The Chop shop first. Then we worry about the others if we don't find him."

"Exactly what I was thinking," responded Kyle, with an even tone.

John looked around momentarily. "We need to find a ride. This Chop shop isn't close."

Kyle looked at John for a moment, contemplating. " Wonder if there is anything in the garage."

John pointed at Kyle accusingly, "Smart idea."

The two men proceeded to the garage, in it there was an SUV. The emblem was missing, but it looked like an Explorer. It was a dark metallic color, not quite black, and the windows were tinted to the darkest shade. It had over sized wheels and low profile tires. It also appeared to be heavier than a normal Explorer. It had a much more substantial suspension, and rode slightly higher than a normal explorer. John could tell immediately that the vehicle had been bulletproofed. That would come in handy. John tried the door, and to his surprise, the door opened, and the keys were sitting in the center console. The two men loaded the weapons in the back of the vehicle and got in the vehicle. Inside, on the visor, there were buttons that looked like they were for a garage door. He tried the first one, and the garage door behind them opened. John pressed the start button and the vehicle came to life. He reached up for the gearshift to see that there wasn't one. After a moment of looking around he noticed a rotary dial that was used for shifting, putting his right foot on the brake, he turned the knob to drive and rolled out of the garage. As he hit the road, John wanted to see what kind of power the vehicle had, so he pushed the gas pedal to the floor. He was expecting the vehicle to be slightly sluggish, but instead, the engine roared and the tires chirped. The speed at which the vehicle accelerated pushed both men back in their seats. Even with the added weight, this vehicle hit 60 miles per hour in about 4.5 seconds. The amount of power put a grin on John's face, when he looked over at Kyle, he was also grinning.

CHAPTER 17

Kyle sat in the passenger seat contemplating a way to calm John down. He had much difficulty in this regard. All of the versions in his mind landed back in the same place, with John more pissed off. Either way, he had to try, just in case.

"John," Kyle began, "How does this end? You have to know that after all of these bodies, and all of this trouble with the law, there isn't a happy ending."

John just glared at him in that way he always got when he wasn't pleased with someone.

Damn this man could stare down a tiger. Kyle thought to himself. He had always been intimidated by John. Even though Kyle had proven on occasion that he was stronger than John, he had never been able to best him in any other area. The last time he tried to wrestle the man to the ground, John had almost separated his shoulder from its socket. Luckily he tapped out before that happened. But Kyle knew, John got a way about him in a fight, he usually didn't stop until he won. Which was great when you were on the same side of the street as him, but if you were against him, there was hell to pay. He had put more than one other officer in the hospital on accident.

"John, I know you don't want to hear this, but someone has to say it. You know I would follow you no matter what, but what exactly is your plan after getting your son back. You won't be able to go back to the force. Hell even I won't be able to. Even if we do get your son back, we will probably just end up in prison. What does that solve?"

John slammed on the brakes in the car, bringing it to a complete stop in the middle of the road. Then he looked back at Kyle with that smoldering look in his eyes.

"I don't care if I have to tear through the the white house itself. I will get my son back. And anyone, I mean ANYONE who stands in my way will die a slow painful death. Do you understand me Kyle. I am not worried about what I need to do after I get my son back. I will live in the friggin jungle if that is what it takes. I will get my son back. Do you understand me? DO YOU KYLE?"

Kyle paused for a moment, slightly terrified of the look in the eyes of the man in front of him. "Crystal clear" Kyle said, barely whispering the words. He could sympathize with John on that matter. That is the only reason he was still sticking around. Nobody screws with another person's family like that, and lives to tell the tale. Kyle was sure about one thing. He wasn't going to try to dissuade John another time. He wasn't sure he would live to tell the tale if he did.

"Glad you see it my way." John said through gritted teeth, and began driving again.

Composing himself, Kyle said, "Well then what is our plan?"

"We will decide that when we arrive" John said.

"Alright" Kyle agreed.

The rest of the car ride was spent in silence. Kyle didn't know how much further he could help John. He was on a path of destruction. And Kyle knew without a shadow of a doubt that John would see this to the end. He would either kill every last person in his way to get to Frank and get his son back. Or he would die trying. Kyle was okay shooting back as long as he was being shot at, but the thought of a killing spree to get to John's son was starting to weigh on him. He wasn't sure his conscience could handle many more deaths. He do his best to see John through getting his son back, but he knew there was a limit to what he could handle and stay sane. Each death he caused weighed on him. He was never good at internalizing it. He had only ever killed three other people before all of this started, and two of them were in the military. The third was when he was a beat cop. He had someone draw on him and he had to put them down. Since this whole mess with John's son had started, he had counted Five bodies on his conscience. That was not a number he ever wanted to reach. In his eyes, confirmed kills were not something that should be bragged about.

As they drove this continued to fester in his mind. As they approached the building Kyle pulled himself free of his thoughts. He couldn't go into this without a clear mind. If he did he was liable to get one or both of them killed. So for the sake of the current mission, he pulled himself away from his thought and worked to clear his mind.

* * *

John and Kyle drove by the chop shop and took stock of the situation. Together they counted seven men out front in various locations. There was no telling how many were inside, but they needed to make sure that they weren't caught again. John parked the SUV about a block down from the chop shop.

"Alright Kyle," John said. "I want you on over watch. I saw a perfect rooftop about two hundred yards from the shop. I understand that you don't wish to be killing people. So with that in mind, I want you to just watch over me and cover me if I need it. "

"No way," Kyle said, "If you get overwhelmed in there, I won't be able to help you. I am going in with you. Whether you want me to or not."

John locked eyes with Kyle, "I am giving you the opportunity to not have to take any more lives."

"I understand that, and I thank you John. But as much as I do not want to take lives, I will not put yours in more danger to lessen my mental burden. I am going in with you."

"Suit yourself." John said.

With that they got to planning. The plan to enter was simple. There were two men at the entrance. Both John and Kyle would take down one man with silenced pistols. Then there were two men roaming throughout the yard. Finally, there were 3 men around the entrance to the building. All of these men had rifles slung to them, so there was no confusing this for a normal wrecking yard slash garage. The goal was to get inside the building without alerting anyone.

After agreeing to the plan, John and Kyle got out of the vehicle and rounded to the back of it. They got out the necessary weapons. Two silenced pistols, and a rifle each. The rifles were not suppressed, and would only be used if issues arose. They both packed 3 magazines of pistol ammunition, and 3 magazines for the rifles. Although the goal was not to use them, being prepared was important. As well as the weapons the also each put a comms unit in their ears.

As they started towards the front gate, Kyle crossed the street and went down the alley. He would be able to come out a little ways further down the street then the entrance and could then come from a different angle then John. John waited just around the corner from the gate.

"Bravo to Alpha, In position." Kyle called over the comms. "Copy," John said, "Wait for my Mark."

Kyle waited patiently as John surveyed to make sure nothing had changed. "Alpha to Bravo, we are good in 3." John called over the radio. Kyle tensed in anticipation. "Two." Kyle heard John say. He peeked around the corner and sighted on the man he was to take down. "One." John said, looking around the corner at his own man.

"Mark!" John said, and both men let one bullet fly from the chamber.

CHAPTER 18

The two men at the gate dropped almost simultaneously. After John and Kyle fired they rushed the gate. Pulling the two men to the side where they wouldn't be seen. Then they checked to make sure no one was watching, and entered the gate, being sure to close it behind them. There were two men roaming down the aisles of vehicles and parts that needed to be taken care of next. John, using hand signals, motioned for Kyle to take the furthermost man. Kyle gave a thumbs up and began to move. John stalked down and aisle parallel to the man he was after. When he found a spot to cut through the two aisles, he did so swiftly and quietly. He double checked to make sure that both men would be out of line of sight to the front door, then he aimed and pulled the trigger. In the same swift motion, he fired one bullet into the side of the head of the man he was after, and caught him before he hit the ground. Then he drug the man off into another pathways between aisles.

Kyle moved quickly toward his target. If he wasn't fast enough, the man would discover John. So Kyle hastened down the pathway. As he approached, the man turned and saw him. However, before the man could do more than squeak, Kyle pulled the trigger. His aim was dead on and the man slumped before being caught by Kyle. Kyle then drug the body of the man off into a corner of the yard and set him down gingerly before closing his eyes and apologizing.

"Bravo to Alpha, Tango two down." Kyle whispered over the comms.

"Copy Bravo, Tango one down." John whispered back.

Kyle and John convened about halfway to the building. They could see the three men lounging near the front door. There were two on the left side and one on the right side. None of the men looked ready to guard the door. They were just sitting there chatting.

"I'll take the two on the left." John said. "You take the one on the right. We will approach from opposite directions and take them down. You approach from behind that van over there." Pointing at a large van in the yard. "I will come from behind the tires on the left. When I say so, take him down."

"Sounds like a plan," Kyle said. With a little bit of regret in his eyes. The two men separated and began making their ways towards their respective destinations.

Arriving behind the van, Kyle peeked around the edge of it. And made sure he could sight hit target.

"Bravo in position." Kyle whispered over comms.

"Copy Bravo," John said. "In 3."

"Two." John said.

Kyle tensed up, he hated doing these things. However, he would not let his feelings put John or his son in any more danger.

"One."

Kyle steeled himself, ready once more, and peeked around the corner again. None of the men had even moved an inch.

"Mark." John said, and both men rounded their hiding spots. John and Kyle fired at roughly the same time. Two of the men dropped, and before the third man could even understand what was happening, he also slumped. Due to the fact that the two men were using subsonic rounds with suppressors, there was very little blood spray. The bullets entered the skulls but did not exit.

Kyle and John took a moment to compose themselves and compose a plan. So far the plan had been silent entry, however, they weren't sure they could enter the building as silently. There was no window on the door, so they were going to have to risk opening it and peeking inside. After conferring for a moment, they decided to enter quickly and hope no one was paying attention. Kyle tried the knob, and it was unlocked. He carefully twisted the knob. John counted down on his fingers and as soon as he put down his last finger, Kyle shoved the door open and John was right behind it. As John entered Kyle noticed two men at the end of the hallway. John quickly and efficiently shot twice. The two men barely understood what was happening before they were dead. They dropped to the floor making two audible thumps. John and Kyle both held their breath, listening for the sound of footsteps down the hallway. There was nothing. Kyle softly closed the door and made sure it was latched. The two men proceeded down the hallway, and at the corner in the hallway where the two men were, they paused. They looked over the men that John had just dropped, the were both wearing full body suits with armor plating in the important areas. Luckily they weren't wearing helmets, otherwise John's bullets would have done little other than alert them to John and Kyle.

"This has to be a trap." Kyle said in a hushed tone.

"I was getting that feeling as well." John replied.

The hallway that they were standing in was a bare white hallway, with one single fluorescent light casting shadows on the floor.

"Should we continue?" Kyle asked cautiously.

"We have to," John started, "We are already in the building, they either know we are here or they don't. Either way, we need to continue."

"Fair point." Kyle agreed.

John stepped forward and quickly peeked around the corner. To his surprise, there was no one there. "All clear." He said, and both men proceeded down the hallway. At the end of the hallway there were two doors. One to the right that was a plain white door, and another at the end of the hallways that was red. The door at the very end looked to be a heavy metal door. They agreed that the larger door must lead to the inside of the shop. The door to the right was probably some sort of office. As John and Kyle approached the door they could see a window in it. So John quickly looked to see if anyone was in there. He didn't immediately see anyone. But that didn't mean there wasn't anyone.

Using the same breaching tactics as before, John and Kyle entered the room and swept through it. However, there was no one in the room. The room looked rather bare. There was one large painting on the wall behind a desk. Opposite the desk was a couch against the wall and two chairs pushed into the desk. On the desk were multiple monitors. Upon further investigation, John and Kyle discovered that the monitors were queued up for the surveillance cameras. There was one showing the three dead men at the front door. The others were showing the inside of the shop. The men were all armed and staring at the large door that led into the hallway.

"Shit!" John said through gritted teeth. "There goes the silent entry we were hoping for."

Kyle looked at John thoughtfully. "These cameras are showing every inch of this place, I don't think he is here. Why don't we just bail?"

John looked at Kyle sharply, "We will leave after I have personally checked every inch of this place. If that means we have to go through all those people, then so be it."

"Alright," Kyle said, "But let's come up with a better plan than just rushing in."

"Agreed." John said.

Kyle began looking around to see what they could use. As he did, he noticed that the large bay doors were powered. And it looked like he had the controls inside the office.

"John," Kyle said, motioning. "I can open the bay doors remotely. That should distract them just enough for us to enter and take them down. But we need to switch to the rifles. Silent went out the window when they saw us coming."

John thought it over for a moment. "It's the best thing we have. Let's run with it."

A few moments later, John stood at the large door in the hallway waiting for Kyle to let him know when to enter.

Kyle watched the cameras and what the men were doing. They appeared to be getting nervous. This was good, if they were nervous they would be jumpy and make mistakes.

"Ready?" Kyle asked.

"Let's do this." John replied.

Kyle hit the buttons that would open the bay doors. Then he watched as the men inside the building started to freak out.

"Now." Kyle shouted.

John entered the shop and immediately took stock and counted the men. At first glance there were 14 men. He instantly sighted and shot one man standing closest to the door. Following that shot with another one in the skull of a man standing about 3 feet from the first. Then two more shots, each finding a target. By this time, some of the others had regained their composure, and began firing. Right after firing the fourth shot John rolled to the right, coming to rest behind the vehicle closest to him.

With all of the focus on John, Kyle entered and followed suit with John's entrance, dropping three men before diving to the left behind another vehicle. He quickly peeked back up firing fast and having one more bullet find its victim. The five men left were hiding behind cars and firing blindly at John and Kyle.

John and Kyle looked at each other to form a plan. Kyle used his hands to suggest that they go around the outside edge of the cars and come around on the 5 men that were left. John nodded his agreement, and they began to move. Both men peeking around the outside edges of the vehicles before moving on. They then quickly moved up the sides and came around on the men. As they each rounded the corners of the cars where the five men were sitting, Kyle said calmly "Drop your guns or die, you have no other options." The look of surprise on the faces of the five men was almost priceless. Then on of the men on Kyle's side tried to point his gun at Kyle. Before he could even aim the rifle, John fired one clean round, spraying blood on the other two that were kneeling there.

"Did that seem like a question," John asked, "Or do I need to tell you again."

The last four men dropped their guns on the ground and held their hands up.

"Much better." John said. "Now who would like to answer some questions?"

One of the men, a skinny young kid who looked like he couldn't be older than 20, spoke up. "I will."

John was surprised that the younger one spoke up first. But then again, the younger ones usually did, because they were more afraid of dying. The other three men glared at the young kid. One of the other ones, a burly man, probably 40, with a long beard, said dryly, "Keep your mouth shut, BOY." There was emphasis on the last word in the sentence.

John turned his rifle around and smashed the but of it directly into the mouth of the man that spoke. There was an audible crack as the man's jaw broke, and a few teeth fell out. As his head recoiled from the impact it smacked into the car that he was sitting against, and lost consciousness. "Anybody else going to try to keep the boy from talking?" John asked. There was silence among the other two men.

"What's your name boy?" John asked.

The younger man looked at the other two nervously, when they didn't say anything, he said, "Richter."

"Alright Richter, do you know who I am?" John asked.

Richter shook his head. "No sir."

John rubbed the bridge of his nose and sighed. "Well then, my name is John Mauser."

When John uttered his name, he watched the realization crawl across Richter's face. As well as the other two men. "Yeah, THAT John Mauser." John said.

"I don't know anything about that." Richter said.

"That look on your face says you know something. So unless you want to look like your friends here." John said, pointing to the dead men on the ground. "You better start talking."

"Look," Richter started, "All I know is, Frank told us he would give $5 million dollars to anyone who brought you to him. Dead or alive. Something tells me, no one is going to be able to collect on that. And that you might take yourself to him."

That gave John pause for a moment. He didn't realize that John had put out a hit on him. It didn't surprise him, but it impressed him how much he was willing to pay.

"Well if he has a hit out on me, then there must be a number or address to collect your money." John said.

Richter shrugged, "He just gave us a number to text a picture to, and told us he would contact us with instructions."

"Well then," John said, "We are going to send a picture."

CHAPTER 19

Frank sat alone in the interrogation room. He had been in there for what he had counted to be about 14 hours. Multiple detectives had been in and out of the room trying to break him. Trying to get him to say something. After almost 15 hours his lawyer had come to stop the interrogations. His lawyer was a man by the name of Lance Brewer. He was one of the best lawyers Frank had ever had, and was not afraid to get his hands dirty. He was a slight man, maybe 3 inches under 6 foot, had blonde hair, and a perpetual grimy look to him. He was not impressive looking, but he made up for his looks with his intelligence and knowledge of the law. He had interrupted the last interrogation, and the detectives had stepped outside to speak with him. The door opened again, and Lance strode in. After looking around the room, he spoke.

"No, this will not do at all. Have you ever heard of Attorney client privilege gentleman? I'd wager not. This room has too many options for you to hear our conversations. No this won't do at all. I need a sealed room, not microphones or cameras. Otherwise, I will be speaking with the judge, and Frank will be released, Do you understand me? Well do you?" He spoke so fast it was hard to keep up with him sometimes, and that nasally voice didn't achieve much either. He looked at the two gentleman that were standing outside the door. Incredulous, he asked, "Well are you two going to get in there and move him, or do I have to do your jobs as well?"

The two men that were standing there paused for a moment longer before moving to unshackle Frank from the chair he sat in. Lance spoke up again," Oh good, you have at least half a brain cell between the two of you."

Frank looked at him with what he hoped was an annoyed look on his face. Seeing that, Lance stopped harassing the two men and let them do their job. After about 3 minutes of shuffling, they sat him down in a chair that was in a room that didn't have the one way glass or the cameras. It was like a really bright closet. Lance sat down in the chair that was pushed against the opposite side of the table. Frank was still handcuffed behind his back, and shacked at the ankles. "Get all this crap off my client," Lance began, "He isn't going to attach his lawyer."

At his request, the men unshackled Franks ankles completely and hand-cuffed his hands to a bar that was welded to the table. "Off with you." Lance said to the two men, waving his hands in a dismissing manner. "I will knock on the door when I need to be let out."

The men rolled their eyes but did as they were asked; leaving the room and shutting the door behind them.

Frank looked at Lance with the same annoyed look as before. "You know I hate when you do that shit." he said flatly. "Now, not that I don't enjoy your company, but why are you here?"

"It worked," Lance said, "I just got a picture of John tied to a chair."

"Excellent," Frank said, "Who sent it?"

"One of the young guys from that shit chop shop you held onto." Lance said.

"Alright, I need you to call him and set up a time and place to bring the detective. Any luck on getting me out of here?"

"Actually, yes, that was the other reason for my visit. I got a judge to sign off on letting you go, as long as you don't attempt to leave the county." Lance said with a smile on his face.

"That is wonderful news," Frank began, "That means you continue to live."

Frank was not a man to be toyed with, when he asked someone to get something done, there was an expectation that they did their best. If their best was not good enough, well that was just too bad. Failure due to lack of ability was just as bad as failure due to lack of effort. Frank did not tolerate failure on any level, if one person could not get it done, he could find someone who could.

"How much did it cost?" Frank asked.

"Actually," lance started, "Nothing. With the detective that found the evidence, and was the star witness, off his rocker, running around killing folks, the judge had no recourse other than to let you go for the time being." He finished that last statement smiling.

"Very well," Frank said coldly, "Get me the hell out of here."

As the two men strode out of the precinct, Frank could feel all of the eyes of the detectives on him. They all wanted to see him face justice, or rather, their form of it. Sure, Frank was technically a criminal, however, he saw what he did as a service. He brought money to Florida that would otherwise not be here. He had drugs being sold throughout the Eastern United States. He was bribing politicians, local government, all of them. He also made sure that he donated to charities, in fact he had his own charity that he ran and funded. He needed an easy money laundering spot. What better a place than a "Non-profit" that he owned indirectly. By being a non-profit, his charity skirted laws on taxes. The other portion of it was the fact that there was no limit to the donations one could receive, very little documentation on who provided the money. Unlike a business that sold goods or performed a service, there was no limit to the laundering potential of a charity. Arriving outside, Frank paused and breathed in deeply. He hadn't been outside in 3 days. A breath of fresh air felt great. His Town car pulled up and him and Lance got inside.

After the doors were closed Frank began, "Now where is the boy being held?"

Lance paused for a moment, "He is being held in the textile factory off 37th avenue. This is the one that you don't officially own.

"Very good, text that boy back and tell him to meet us at the warehouse near the Wharf. And then make damn sure we have enough security there." Frank stated.

"Are you going to be there as well?" Lance asked.

"Of course not, but there needs to be plenty of cameras throughout the building." Frank said.

"Yes sir," Lance began, "I will make it happen."

CHAPTER 20

After John got Richter to send the picture to the number that was provided, the two men left the rest of the men with the expectation that they keep they keep quiet. They made slightly veiled threats that they would never follow up on. John and Kyle both knew that they would be walking into a trap at the very least. So if the men at the chop shop said something, it would not change the outcome.

About 5 hours after they sent the picture to the number provided, they got a response with an address a date and a time. Nothing else. When John tried to send a response, the number came back disconnected. *Smart,* John thought. That way the phone couldn't be traced after giving the meeting time and place. The meeting was at an abandoned warehouse, scheduled for 2 days later late in the evening. The message did not have a number, it had simply read "late evening, wait for further instruction."

John and Kyle knew they didn't have a lot of time to plan, so they wanted to drive to the location right away and scout it. As it was approaching evening they arrived a couple blocks from the location to begin scouting. There were not a lot of large buildings to be on top of, which was good and bad. This meant that there were no significant vantage points to watch from. This also meant that Frank had no significant vantage points. Upon further investigation, there were 3 locations from which a person could provide over watch.

John and Kyle then spent the next few hours scouting the locations for over watch. After finishing the first two buildings, they were approaching the third one when John noticed that it looked like someone had already been on the rooftop. There was a hideout that was camouflaged to look like the surrounding building. This meant that Frank was planning an ambush, which both men expected, and that they were already set up for it. However, this was also good news. The fact that they were set up on this roof most likely meant that the others were not going to be set up on before the meeting. This meant that they could wait for Frank's man to show up on this rooftop and subdue him before the meeting. Based on past events John expected the man to show up about 12 hours before the meeting. Which would then give them plenty of time to go check out the building, and get back before Frank's over watch. They used this time wisely, scoping out the meeting place, and finding that it was rigged with about 15 cameras. These were undoubtedly to record John either being gunned down, or for evidence to use against him in the future.

When John and Frank checked out the cameras, they noticed that they were hardwired with a battery backup in case the electricity failed. John and Frank sabotaged each of the cameras in a way that made it look as though they had not been tampered with. They pulled the backup batteries, and after a run to the store, they swapped the camera's internal memory chips with ones that would not be able to store more than roughly one minute of footage. This ensured that even if they were to notice the batteries missing, they would not be able to record much footage. After completing their recon and sabotaging the cameras, they returned to the rooftop.

They managed to return to the rooftop before the man that had set up the hiding spot. Then they began the long wait for the man that was going to show up at some point in time. John was sitting there staring off into space, when he finally drifted off to sleep.

John looked around. He was in his room, still laying in bed. Kari came up to him and kissed him softly. "Hey sleepy, you better get up or you are going to be late."

"Late for what?" John asked, trying to shake the fuzz from his mind.

"Late to save me from Frank" Kari said softly.

Did he just hear what he thought he had. "What was that?" He asked.

"Late to work silly." Kari said, giggling. That wasn't what he heard the first time. He knew it, but he couldn't put his finger on why. Something was off, his head was still fuzzy and he couldn't hear correctly. The giggle from Kari seemed to

echo in the room. What was happening. He reached out for Kari and grabbed her arm. That felt real enough, "What is going on?" He asked forcefully. Kari grinned back, and evil grin that he had never seen from her. "Nothing silly, you are just late. Always late." She giggled again, and again it seemed to echo in the small room.

"Kari, where is Lane?" John asked frantically.

"He is gone, silly." More giggling.

"What do you mean gone?" John asked more urgently. "Where is he?"

"They took him with them" Kari said again. Giggle echoing in the small room.

His head was still so damn fuzzy, he couldn't figure out what was going on. "Late, late, late, late." Kari said staring at him. Still with that evil grin on her face. "Always too late." John was starting to spiral. "Better wake up before you are too late again."

"What are you talking about?" John said.

"Wake up," Kari said in a slightly distorted voice.

"I am awake," John said.

"No you aren't," Kari started, "WAKE UP!" She shouted in his face, but it wasn't her voice, who's was it. It took him a moment. That was Kyle's voice.

John snapped awake with a start. Kyle was right in front of him, with his hands on John's shoulders. "You awake?" Kyle asked. "It's almost time."

John could feel the tears streaming down his face. "Yeah, yeah, I'm good." he said, shaking his head a little more. Blessedly that cleared his mind. In the dream his mind felt so fuzzy. Those dreams were getting more vivid each time he slept. Which made things worse. It meant even if he fell asleep, it wasn't going to be restful, and was going to be terrible.

A few minutes later, John and Kyle got the notification that their geofence on the stairs was triggered. That meant that the over watch for Frank's men was coming up the stairs. Only one person crossed the trigger point, that was good. John and Kyle got into position and waited for the man to come out the door. When he did, they pounced. He was caught off guard by them. Kyle ran out of the corner and hit the man in the back of the knees with a metal pipe, making him collapse. The John came up behind him and put him in a choke hold. He squeezed until the man stopped wriggling, which lasted a surprising amount of time. When he was unconscious, John and Kyle carried him back down one flight of stairs and tied him to a chair, so they could interrogate him.

John slapped the man hard enough to wake him up from his stupor. When the man woke up, he was notably confused. He looked around the room, not speaking, but slowly recognizing what was happening. He looked at his wrists and then down at his ankles, noticing he was tied to a chair. "Hey there sleepy head." John said sarcastically. "How's your day going?"

The man locked eyes with john and in a flat tone said, "I've had better."

"Well that's good, if you had had worse days I wouldn't think this would work." John said this as he pulled the knife off of his waistband and held it toward the man threateningly.

"You really think I am afraid of a knife?" The man asked accusingly. "Look, I just want to go home, let's not do this shit. I know eventually you will either get your information or kill me. So what do you want to know?"

John grinned, and put away his knife. "Smart choice. How many people are arriving down at the warehouse?"

"Thirty or Forty," The man said, without emotion.

"How well armed will they be?" Kyle piped up from the corner of the room.

"Very well." The man said. Again devoid of any emotion. "Frank wants you dead, and he is going to tape it. If it somehow goes south for his men, he wants the footage to send to the police. It's lose lose for you."

"We knew about the cameras," John said. "They won't be recording much. Last question. Will Frank be there?"

The man in the chair thought about that for a moment. "You know, I knew this wasn't going to go well for us. After everything, Frank still thinks he is dealing with an amateur."

"That doesn't answer my question." John said, reaching to his belt for the knife.

The man watched as John's hand rested on the hilt of the knife. "No, he won't be there." He said, returning to looking at John's face. "He planned on watching it remotely."

"Wonderful," John said, visibly angry, "We will just have to give him a show." He looked at the man, "Where is your car?"

The man obliged with the location of his car, and John began to tell Kyle about his plan.

CHAPTER 21

John waited on the roof while Kyle got both vehicles ready. He moved their vehicle to a clear escape location, they set up the other vehicle with a hefty amount of explosives. Then the two men waited for everyone to start arriving. Although Frank thought he was dealing with an amateur, John could tell that he thought he was dangerous. Over fifty different people showed up, all very heavily armed. They waited for everyone to be in place, then set their plan in motion. Kyle started the vehicle with the explosives and set it to roll slowly toward the warehouse. John was on the roof with a rifle waiting. For some reason, the sniper had incendiary rounds in his arsenal, and this would pay off. John watched the car roll slowly toward the warehouse with no driver in it. The windows in this car were tinted to a level that it was not clear who or what was inside the car. This was common for men that worked for Frank, as it meant they wouldn't be spotted by cameras inside their cars.

The people in the warehouse got a clue that something was wrong when the vehicle didn't stop as it approached them. However, they were much too slow to react, and their immediate reaction was to start shooting at the car. John aimed the rifle and let one round fly towards the car.

The resulting explosion, was, well, beautiful. John watched as the round he shot struck the car, and set off the explosives inside. It was like watching a flower bloom in a sped up video. He watched the fireball expand outward and envelope everything. As that was happening, the shock-wave hit everything. The building that he was standing on shook as though there was an earthquake happening. That was the single largest explosion he had ever witnessed. It was a good thing that he was wearing ear plugs, because the sound from the explosion shattered most of the windows in the surrounding buildings. After the initial explosion and flame the mushroom cloud roiled upward in a beautiful fashion. Continuing to watch, it was clear to John that there were going to be no survivors, this was reinforced by the fact that the explosion collapsed the building that everyone was in. It was now just a pile of rubble on the ground. John quickly descended the stairs in the building and made his way to the alleyway the Kyle was waiting at in their vehicle. He threw everything in the back and hopped inside. Kyle threw the car into drive and began to make his way away from the scene. He wanted to make sure that they were as far away from this place as possible when the police arrived. Which was going to be very shortly.

Kyle drove the back-roads away from the explosion in a zig zag pattern. He wanted to make sure it did not look as though they were coming from the explosion. As he was driving, Kyle looked at John, "Jesus man, did we have to use all of the explosives that guy had? We just killed well over fifty people with one bullet."

John eyed Kyle, "I know very well what we just did, and I feel no remorse. They all worked for Frank, and they would've killed us if they had the chance. Plus, I fired the round, so you have a clear conscience."

"Jesus John, how far are we going to go on this? How far is too far? You know there is no coming back from this." Kyle said, looking upset.

"I tell you what Kyle, if you no longer have the stomach for this, I will do it myself. You can go act like you were on vacation somewhere. They won't have any way to tie you to this, and you can go back to being a cop. But in case you are wondering, I will not stop until I have my son in my arms and Frank is dead. That is a promise to you and anyone else who questions how far I would go. I would kill the president himself to get to my son."

"Christ John, I know you love your son, and that you want revenge, but is this the way to do it? To go on a rampage through the city, leaving bodies in your wake?"

"Kyle, I won't tell you again, I will go through anyone to get to Frank. I will kill everyone that has a hint of an association. Stop the car and get out. I'll finish this myself."John said this last bit almost yelling. He was shaking with anger. Kyle stopped the car but didn't get out.

"John, I am on your side, I just worry if you are going to hit a point of no return. Is it worth it to get your son back, only to then be thrown in prison for how many murders now? You are no use to Lane dead or in prison. So what is your plan?" Kyle tried to remain as calm as possible and appeal to John's self preservation instincts.

"I have already thought about it. I can't go back to being a cop. My son and I will be fugitives, but we will be fugitives together. That is all I care about. The only thing I have left is my son. As long as I have him, I don't care what happens." John said this last bit with tears streaming down his face. He was crying, and Kyle understood. "That is why I keep telling to to back out. If you follow me down this path, there is no going back. We have already gone too far. I can bear all of the blame so far, but If we see this to completion you will also be a fugitive. You will no longer be able to return to normal life. Kyle you are my partner, and my best friend, and I do not take that lightly. I expect to end up on Americas most wanted list. I do not want you on there with me unless you are one hundred percent invested. So before you say yes to continuing to help me, understand something. You will be a fugitive, and you will no longer be on the right side of the law. Do not make your choice lightly." As he was saying this spiel he calmed down. He looked at Kyle with glassed over eyes. They were haunted eyes that showed he was not lying about his intention. He would go through anything and anyone to get his son back. Kyle understood this, having lost his brother in Afghanistan. Kyle struggled with this decision more than he thought he should have. His first instinct was to continue to help John. However, he knew John was telling the truth. He more on the side of law than John was, that was why he never went undercover with John. He was no good at breaking the law. However, without John, he felt he would have nothing left to fight for. He wasn't married, and didn't have children. John was his closest friend and after 15 years of working with John, they worked like a well oiled machine. Finally he came to the conclusion that he had already gone too far to go back, and he was going to continue. "I'm in it all the way." Kyle said to John.

"Alright then, I need you to stop questioning me, we finish this my way. And there are going to be more bodies. Do you understand?" John said this with an authoritative tone that made Kyle think of boot camp. "Got it." He said, and put the vehicle back in gear.

CHAPTER 22

"DAMMIT, DAMMIT, DAMMIT, DAMMIT." Frank shouted as he pounded his fist on the table. "How did this go so wrong?" He asked no one in particular. He looked around the room at the group of people in front of him. "Is no one going to speak. You," Frank said with ferocity, as he pointed at a man among the front of his group. "You were in charge of recon, were you not?"

The man stammered for a moment, " I was sir. The only position that could be used for over-watch was taken into account. But it would appear they got to the man I sent there."

Frank looked at him with hate. "You only sent one man to over-watch?" He asked with a sickeningly calm voice.

The man knew he was in deep water, "Well yes sir, you said you wanted every person in the warehouse. So I did not spare any other than the one."

"Are you saying this is my fault?" Frank asked.

The man began to speak, however, before he could get a word out Frank fired one bullet out of his pistol. Striking the man square between the eyes, killing him instantly. Frank preferred to use subsonic rounds as they left less of a mess when killing someone. The man fell forward almost in slow motion and hit the ground with the thump of a limp body.

"Anyone else have any wise words on how we failed?" Frank asked angrily. After a moment of silence he responded to himself. "Good, everyone go!" He said, waving his hand absently. "And someone get this garbage out of here." Motioning to the spot where the dead man was bleeding on the concrete.

As everyone was exiting the room Frank stopped one man. "Oh,.. Charles, hold up for a moment." Charles was one of the men that saw to his staffing needs. He was a stout fellow. Had dark brown eyes, that almost looked black. That coupled with the bald head gave Charles the look of a dangerous man. Even with his meager height of only 5 foot 7 inches. He also had tattoos covering most exposed skin on his body. He did like to express himself with ink. "I need you to round up every mercenary we know. I want John dead before the end of tomorrow." Charles stopped and looked at Frank, incredulous. "Sir, don't you think that after this last display that may be a little difficult?"

"I don't care if it is difficult, make it happen. And I expect I do not have to tell you what happens when people fail me, DO I?" Frank said this, motioning to the body still lying on the floor.

"No sir, consider it done." Charles said curtly as he exited the room.

Frank sat alone for some time brooding on his mistakes leading up to this mess. After a couple of minutes the cleaning crew came in to take care of the dead man lying on his floor. He thought about his lax trusting of Jake, or rather, John. He was taken by surprise that someone was able to climb through his organization so thoroughly and efficiently. He had been to relaxed. He thought himself untouchable by the Miami PD. He had about half the precinct on the payroll. So he generally knew every rat they tried to stuff into his home. They had kept this one on pretty tight wraps, as it seemed no one knew about it. However, when they arrested him, he knew that the man was a cop, and thankfully the cops that took him to the precinct were on his payroll and told him who John was and even where he lived. He gave them the orders to pass onto his men. They were to go into John's house and kill any family he had, however, Frank had a set of rules that even he followed. He never killed children. He did not feel he was an evil man because of this one rule he followed, and made everyone in his organization follow. Never kill children. There were many men he had killed because they had harmed or killed children. He did not like having women killed, as he felt it was not a chivalrous thing to do, but sometimes it was a necessary evil, a means to an end. He had wanted to send a message to John, he did not realize just how ferocious and hard to kill the man would be.

After a few minutes of brooding, Lance came into the room holding something and looking scared. "S.. Sir, they texted the phone again."

"What?" Frank asked urgently, "Let me see that phone."

Lance handed the phone over to Frank. As he opened it he saw that there was one message from the same number that had been previously used. The message read, "Any other smart ideas?" This enraged Frank, not only had they killed all of the men at that warehouse, now they were taunting him. Frank looked up at Lance. "Go. Get. Me. The Child." He said through clenched teeth. He was going to finish this if he had to do it himself.

A few minutes later, Lance came strolling in, practically dragging the child. "Jeez, I hate children." Lance said as he deposited the boy in front of Frank.

Frank took the boy and put him in a chair near his desk. He then took a picture and sent it to the number that was texting him. The message read " 37th and Lex. 10 am. Come alone or the boy dies."

After sending the message, Frank instructed Lance to gather up all of the men, including those that Charles was getting, and bring them all to the factory. He would have so many men at the factory it would be impossible for John to exit alive.

CHAPTER 23

John and Kyle were sitting in the car in an alleyway far away from the warehouse that they blew up. Neither had slept much. John kept having the recurring nightmares of Kari, where he was unable to get to her in time. Unable to help her, unable to touch her. The nightmares were getting worse and worse. Every time he fell asleep, the nightmares were there. He couldn't save Kari, and it seemed the nightmares were telling him he wouldn't be able to save Lane. However, he would not give up. As he had told Kyle, this was only going to end one of two ways. With him dead, or with Frank dead. There was no other choice in his mind.

John and Frank had talked it over and thought that trying to taunt Frank was going to be their best course of action. John had just eliminated over fifty men that Frank employed. There were going to be more, but he knew this would piss Frank off. So they then sent a message to the number that they had saved in the phone that they took off of Richter. The message was simple, but if Frank had access to it, John was sure it would anger him to the point of doing something stupid. The message read, "Any other smart ideas?" Plain, and straight to the point. No blame, no admonition of guilt, just a simple message. They had been waiting for nearly an hour for a response, both men sitting in the vehicle tense as could be.

"So where do we go after everything?" Kyle asked absently.

"I hadn't put much thought into the matter." John responded without looking at Kyle. " Honestly my sole focus has been on Lane. I have to get him back. Whatever I do after that is inconsequential to me. As long as I have my boy."

Kyle chewed on that response for a while. " Well then, lets get your boy." He said after a time.

They sat in silence for a little while longer before a response came across on the phone. "37th and Lex. 10 am. Come alone or the boy dies." Along side the message was a picture of Lane. It did not appear they had harmed him much, however he had been crying. This just incentivized John more.

John looked and Kyle and then showed him the message. "It's a trap John." Kyle said. John paused a moment. " You are damn right it is. But not for me. It's going to be a trap for them." John was a deadly man when provoked. He had already proven this multiple times. John could see that Kyle was worried about this going sideways for him. However, John was at peace. He knew there were only two outcomes. It was either going to end with him dying or him getting his boy.

John and Kyle had roughly 4 hours to plan for the meeting. The message was very clear that John should come alone, however, he was going to have Kyle be over-watch if at all possible. Since it was yet to be known that they were driving the vehicle, John and Kyle drove by the location a couple of times. In driving by a few times, they noticed there was very little area for over-watch. Across from the location, which by all looks was a textile factory, there were a few houses, and a church. The Church would have been perfect, however it was a simple church without a second story. This meant that John was going to be going in without backup.

* * *

"John, you are going to die." Kyle said in a pleading voice. "There is no over-watch, you are going in without being able to see inside, it a no win situation. Please man, don't do this."

John looked at Kyle with pain in his eyes. "I am already committed to this. There is no stopping me. If my son is in there I am going to get him. And I am going to kill anyone that stands in my way."

Kyle decided to stop trying to talk him out of it. "Alright, look, the car is bulletproof. So use that to your advantage. They are probably not expecting you to be in a car like this. So you should have the element of surprise."

"Good thought," John started. "They are probably going to light up the car the moment I come to a stop. So I sit in the car a moment before getting out."

Kyle and John also stopped by an electronics store and picked up a wireless GoPro camera. They were going to put this on the dash of the car, and have it transmit to a phone that they bought. Kyle was going to hold onto the phone and turn it over to the cops if this went sideways for John. That was there was hopefully some evidence against Frank. They tested out the camera to make sure that it was properly transmitting, and then set it to record. John looked at Kyle with a small smirk on his face. "Let's have some fun." He said, and reached out to grasp Kyle's hand and pulled him towards him in a half hug. "Stay safe friend." Kyle said.

CHAPTER 24

John pulled up towards the factory and could see all of the people inside the building on the ground level. As he pulled in the building he saw what he was expecting. Arranged all

around the top level of the building were men with rifles, all kinds of different rifles. He thought he could even see some heavy machine guns. This impressed him, was he that much of a threat? Did Frank really fear him so much that he was willing to go to such lengths to kill him. Instantly he knew the answer to the question. Of course Frank was afraid of what he could do. He has single handedly killed hundreds of Franks men. Upon the thought of causing such a reaction in a man made John smile. He had left Kyle in a building down the street with one rifle to sneak up and provide over-watch. However with the way this building was laid out, there was not going to be much help that Kyle could provide. John realized, with a sudden feeling, there was only one way he was going to get out of this. And that was to survive the hail of bullets and kill everyone. An impossible task if you asked anyone else. However, nothing was going to stand in his way.

After looking around and seeing everyone with guns in their hands, he focused forward again and noticed Frank, standing there with Lane on the ground in front of him. He saw Lanes face, and he knew the score. Frank wanted Lane to see what happened to his father. He wanted to show the child what happened to people who defied him. He also wanted to show John that he was willing to kill him in front of his child. John brought the car to a stop and stared at

Frank. The front windshield was slightly tinted, but John knew Frank could see his face, and for just a moment, it looked as if Frank faltered. John knew he had murder in his eyes, there was no denying that. After recovering from his hesitation Frank threw his arm and hand forward in a motion that most likely signaled everyone to start shooting.

* * *

As Frank stood there with the boy in front of him waiting for John to show up he recounted everything, and to his math, had credited that there was no way John would make it out of this warehouse alive. He had dozens of men on each side balcony of the warehouse. Frank wanted to be certain that if John showed up, there was no way he would leave. On each side he had set up men with assault rifles. Pulling this string had been difficult. He had free access to weapons that he needed, however, when he needed 50 rifles in such a short amount of time, it took some effort. However, like everyone in his employ, it was made clear that his supplier for such arms was not to fail him. The man, Everett, had complained and whined, but in the end managed to get all of the rifles Frank needed. He even managed to provide Frank with a couple of M249's. Military grade Light Machine Guns. With that he managed to scrounge up two M2 Browning machine guns. They had limited ammunition as .50 caliber BMG ammunition was hard to get a hold of. As Frank stood there and accounted for everything, he was sure this would go his way.

Frank had been waiting there for about half an hour when one of his spotters let him know that a vehicle was pulling up to the warehouse. Frank signaled for the doors to be opened, and moments later, a vehicle pulled in. This was a very nice looking vehicle, that also had the appearance of being armored. That surprised Frank, as he didn't think that John would have the ability to pull those kinds of strings. However, with the kind of firepower that Frank was packing, it didn't matter much if John had shown up in a tank.

As he pulled the car in slowly, Frank could see the man looking around the warehouse appraisingly. There was a hint of shock and surprise in the face that then looked at him. The look that John gave him was one of cold blooded murder. That startled Frank as no one had ever given him that look before. Not a single person alive had ever scared Frank, except for this man today. Frank felt a chill run through him, as he second guessed if he in fact did have enough firepower. After a moment of disbelief, he caught himself, and reassured by the amount of people he had, steadied himself for the task at hand. Frank lifted his left hand and signaled, The signal that everyone in the warehouse was waiting for. That signal said open fire.

* * *

As promised, Kyle snuck into a halfway over-watch position to watch John approach this ambush. His position was not great, as there were no great positions. However, due to the fact that he was on the ground floor, he would be able to see quite a bit as soon as they opened the doors. He watched as John pulled up in the car and waited for the doors to open. As the doors rolled back, Kyle saw the ambush that John was driving into. There was no getting him out of it, and he silently cursed. John was screwed, well and truly. However, he was going to provide the best over-watch someone can, as he watched he made note of the heavy and light machine guns on the balcony above where he could see Frank standing. He watched as Frank faltered for a moment, then suddenly gather his courage again. He watched Frank's arm go in the air, and with a decisive motion, signal to his men to start firing. Kyle then quickly sighted on one of the heavy machine gunners.

CHAPTER 25

As John sat in the vehicle he watched Frank give the order. It was the order that he was hoping Frank would not give right away, as he wanted to talk to the man. However, Frank wasn't taking any chances, and now John knew that.

As the bullets started flying, John silently cursed, however at the same time was impressed by his luck. The car he was sitting in was made to withstand just about everything conventional handheld weapons could throw at it. The bullets started hitting the car in a deafening fashion. John watched in horror as the two heavy machine gunner's cocked their weapons and sighted in. However, before either of them could begin to fire, the head of the one on the right exploded. This snapped John out of his daze and he threw the vehicle in reverse and stomped on the accelerator. The second man began firing his weapon, and the bullets packed a massive punch. His entire windshield spider-ed. John could tell immediately that it would not withstand that kind of abuse for very long. Luckily as he was accelerating, he noticed the second man slump after only a couple seconds. Damn Kyle really was worth his weight in gold on this endeavor. Just as he exited the building John threw the vehicle sideways, exposing the side to everyone. He climbed in the backseat and grabbed his rifle, and opened the door on the passenger side of the vehicle that faced outward.

John rolled out of the vehicle and put his back to it to give himself a moment to take in his surroundings and make sure that his weapon was loaded. He grabbed all of the extra ammunition for his M4 that he could carry. He holstered the 1911 on his side along with all of the ammunition for that. It was go time. He quickly counted to himself how many shots Kyle had provided. *Crack,* he saw the muzzle flash from Kyle's rifle once more, and marked it at 6. If he didn't start firing soon, they were going to be able to track him. The back of the SUV was right up against the side of the building so John skirted to the back and quickly peeked through a small gap to catch a glimpse. Everyone inside was firing wildly at the SUV. John was really impressed with the quality of the vehicle.

Seeing a handful of men through the gap, John shouldered his M4, and sighted around the corner. The people that he could see still hadn't noticed where he was. He quickly dropped one, then two, and then a third. Each round finding its home without issue. The three men he fired at dropped dead, one of them fell over the railing. The chaos that was ensuing was actually going to help him, as they were not paying attention to where the bullets were coming from. He rounded the end of the SUV again, and caught two more men off guard. By his accounting that put the total up to eleven between him and Kyle. There were at least fifty men in the building before when he showed up.

He saw Kyle's muzzle flash again, and counted that as another hit. Kyle did not miss targets standing still. Counting that as 12 down, John peeked around the back of the SUV again, seeing two more men, he let loose another 2 rounds. The first one found its home quickly, however the second man was already looking and narrowly escaped his fate. The man fired back and missed John by mere inches. He felt the air on his face that was displaced by the bullet. John let loose a volley of rounds to suppress the man and hopefully catch him off guard. This tactic did work and John caught the man in the left shoulder. This caused him to stumble and John fired once more to finish him off.

Continuing his count, marking the last man as 13 dispatched, John decided it was time to move. There were still a lot of men left to handle, however with Kyle's suppression, John was certain he would be able to move without being caught. He chanced a glance over the vehicle and saw that most of the men were distracted. With about one third of the men now dead, they were in disarray trying to figure out how their plan had gone to shit so fast. John could see the look of fear in their eyes. He took advantage of this confusion and rushed into the warehouse. As he entered he saw three things. The first was that the layout of the warehouse was designed so that there were stairs on either side leading up. However, they were not covered, and were sure to mean John's demise if he tried to climb them while getting shot at. The second item that caught his attention was that the men noticed him rushing in and were quickly trying to recover. The third and final thing John noticed was Frank at the other end of the building running away with Lane over his right shoulder.

As John proceeded into the warehouse, he pushed himself to run as fast as he could and dove behind a concrete wall on the bottom floor until he could find a better way upstairs to deal with the men at the top. As he dove toward the concrete, the *Crack* of a rifle sounded in his ears, and momentarily filled him with dread. However, as he rolled to a stop, he realized he had not been shot at, and that the sound was from Kyle's rifle. *That equals 14.* John thought to himself making sure he would not lose count. After Kyle's shot, John heard the fire of automatic weapons and saw as dust started to fly up around him. The concrete wall was thankfully over an inch thick, however, he knew it would not stop the bullets for long. He peeked around the end of the wall with his rifle and quickly dispatched two men that were not entirely focused on him. *16 down.* He thought. John looked around to try and find anything that may help him out of this predicament. *Crack.* John noted another man down as the sound of Kyle's rifle struck. Looking around frantically, John noticed a fire extinguisher on the ground. He scrambled over and quickly picked up the canister. He thanked an unknown god as he realized it was full. He had never seen anyone shoot a fire extinguisher, and he hoped it would create the needed confusion for him to be able to get to the stairs behind the men and get up top before they started firing at him.

Counting down from three, John readied himself. Whether or not the canister provided the needed smoke screen, he was going to have to make a run for it.

3.... John was quickly getting ready to throw the canister, and was figuring out the best angle at which to do it. 2.... John tested the weight of the canister to make sure he would be able to throw it the needed distance. He was sure he could. 1... He checked the bolt on his rifle, and then, he threw it.

* * *

Kyle was watching and trying to pick off people as John ran into the warehouse. But he knew he needed to conserve his ammo. He had a limited amount of rounds, and did not want to waste them unnecessarily. He saw a man about to shoot John as he started to dive behind a concrete wall and took his shot, quickly dropping the man that had sighted on John. Kyle watched as John peeked around the end of the concrete wall and fired 2 rounds. As John pulled back behind cover, Kyle noticed a man reading to throw something at John. So with a deftly placed shot, Kyle dropped that man as well. Kyle then watched as John grabbed something. He was not certain, but through the scope he thought it was a fire extinguisher. Kyle watched with fascination as John paused for a couple moments, and then threw the fire extinguisher. While it was in mid air, John quickly stood and started to run. Mid stride, Kyle watched as John twisted and let loose one round that struck the canister. As the bullet struck, the canister began to spin and spew fire retardant in a circular cloud, momentarily obscuring John from sight. Kyle took this time to maintain the confusion and try to take out as many of the men as possible.

He fired once, then twice, and then a third time. All in quick succession, and each finding the intended target. As he pulled the bolt back for a fourth shot, Kyle heard footsteps behind him and a shadow descended over him. He heard a voice say, "Put down the rifle", in a southern accent.

* * *

As the canister left John's hand, he started to run, only pausing slightly to turn and fire a round at the canister. The result couldn't have been any better in John's eyes. The fire extinguisher began to spin and spew its contents in a circular pattern, covering a large area and obscuring his movement.

As John ran towards the stairs, he heard Kyle's rifle shoot three more times, then stop. *Odd,* He thought as he reached the stairs and began to ascend them. He decided not to pay it much attention and to focus on what lay before him. As he reached the top of the stairs, John noticed only one man paying attention to them. The man was waiting, but luckily was not a great shot. He fired once in John's direction, barely missing him. John then brought his rifle to bear and shot the man twice in the chest. As the body hit the floor, the others around the man started to turn. John recognized that although he would be able to take down a number of them before they shot, if he did not move, they would catch him. So he decided to drop his rifle and let the sling catch it. As he let go, he darted forward, and drew his sidearm.

John reached the closest man before he had time to bring his own weapon to bear, and from his hip, fired three shots into the mans chest. As he fired, John grabbed the man and turned him in the direction of the man that was about to fire. As the man fired at John, John let the body of the man he was holding absorb the rounds, and then he fired twice at the shooter and caught him between the eyes. Then John quickly disengaged the body of the man he was holding and rolled backwards to avoid the next shooters aim. As John dropped he fired once at the man that was doing the same at him. Rolling backwards and ending upright, John quickly realized his bullet had found its intended target. With the group of four men taken care of, John quickly assessed his situation. With the three shots Kyle fired and the four men he had just taken down, that equaled 23. He could see that more men were coming towards him, and so he quickly counted in his head how many rounds were left in his pistol. John's 1911 used double stack magazines and thus held 14 rounds. That meant there were still 8 left in the gun. He was not certain how many rounds he had fired out of the M4, however, he was not entirely worried as it held 30 rounds and he had taken the liberty of taping two mags together to make the swap faster.

CHAPTER 26

"I've got him." Frank heard as the radio crackled. As the conflict had started, Frank made off with the boy to make sure neither of them were to get shot by accident. Frank was not above killing children, however, if the boy was going to die, it was not going to be from a stray round. Frank wanted to make sure that the leverage he had on John stayed intact as long as possible.

"That's very good. Bring him to the back of the warehouse." Frank replied over the radio. He smiled to himself that he had seen fit to have a man stationed in the only building that provided an over-watch position into the warehouse. However, Frank had the man wait until the conflict started to go up to the roof. This was to ensure he would be able to surprise anybody assisting John, and not the other way around. Frank realized his mistake from the first warehouse. The man that was meant to provide over-watch had been caught off guard. He wouldn't allow it to happen again.

"Yessir." The radio crackled once more. The man Frank had used for the job was one of his most trusted enforcers. He was from Georgia, and he was no small human. The man looked to weigh in at roughly 300 pounds. However, with his bulk, he was still quite stealthy. Frank grinned to himself once more as he felt his plan coming together. He would let John fight through the men he had brought. They were to try and kill him, but from what Frank had recently found out. John was no easy man to kill. This meant that he had a backup plan, in the unlikely event that John was able to make it past the men. He felt it was unlikely, but he was not a man to be easily caught off guard, and thus he always had a contingency plan.

Where Frank was going to be taking the boy and John's accomplice was below the warehouse. Frank had seen fit to have this warehouse outfitted with, what was, essentially a bomb shelter. It was a concrete bunker about 20 feet underground. This was his final plan.

As Frank descended the stairs, the boy started to fight him. He was kicking and screaming, and just making it difficult for Frank to descend the stairs. Frank paused about halfway down and looked the boy in the eyes. "Either you stop fighting me, or..." Frank paused for dramatic effect. " I will make you."

Frank could see the fear in the boys eyes. As he picked him up to keep going the boy did nothing. He just silently wept as they came to the bottom of the stairs. The commotion up above took on a muffled tone, and he could barely hear anything.

Frank pushed open the door and waited for the other two to show up. He did not have long to wait. About 5 minutes later, the other two men arrived at the bottom of the stairs and entered the room.

CHAPTER 27

John advanced quickly towards the next group of men. Even as they were turning to face him. As he was advancing he fired three rounds. Two in the chest of the closest man, and one in the leg of the man behind the first. The first man fell to the ground as John reached the group. John saw as the second man started to bring his rifle around, even laying on the ground. Just before the man shot, John kicked the barrel of the rifle, causing the second man to miss his shot. John took the moment to fire one round into the left eye of the man he was standing over. He had no time to pause as the third man in line began to fire at him. Sidestepping the first round and advancing the distance between them John fired at the man, even as he was firing at John. John's bullet hit home, spraying blood at the men behind his target. As he saw his round hit home, John felt a searing pain, like that of a hot iron, on his left thigh. He knew he had been shot, but had no time to think about it, as there were still at least twenty men in front of him. His only advantage being there were too many of them confined to all fire at him at once.

The fourth and closest man was too close to shoot at John, and vice a versa. John holstered his pistol quickly, so he would not lose it. Instead of trying to fire, the man lunged at John. He first threw a punch from his right side, fast enough that it was simply a blur in John's vision. John pulled back and felt a rush of air as the man's fist passed in the spot that his face had just been. John took advantage of the miss and grabbed the man's wrist with his right hand and used the man's momentum to throw him onto the floor. His head hit the floor first stunning him, then John twisted the man's wrist to the right and pulled on his arm, at the same time he lifted his leg and stomped down on the man's shoulder. The sound was still audible in the chaos, and was a sickening sound, followed by the scream of the man. John let go of his wrist as four more, this time with knives, advanced toward him.

In this John had a slight advantage as the walkway was not wide enough for them to surround him easily. Also, as John had hoped, by dealing with the last man in such a gruesome manner, they were slightly hesitant to attack him. Their hesitation was all the initiative John needed. John feigned at the man closest to his, and as he pulled away, John thrust his right leg at the second man. John's foot caught the man off guard, and the blow made him stumble backwards several feet gasping for air,before falling to the ground and dropping his knife. With his movement, John had tried to pay no attention to his left leg, however momentarily after kicking, his leg gave out and he stumbled, barely keeping his feet underneath him. The first man which he had feigned at had gathered himself by then, and thrust his knife at John with his right hand. John noticed the action and began to sidestep to his right even as he brought his right hand up to catch the attacker's arm. John caught the man's wrist and began to push it away from his body as he pivoted. Bringing his left arm up, John took hold of the knife as as he finished the rotation and used the man's momentum to throw him at the other two. John took their momentary confusion to draw his 1911 once more and used each of his last three rounds to dispatch the men in front of him.

Turning his attention to the others, John made a show of dropping the magazine out of the gun and inserting the new one. When it clicked into place, John pressed down on the slide release, and allowed it to slide into place, as it did the *schrack* sound was audible. After witnessing John dispatch the last two groups of men with relative ease, most of the men dropped their weapons and scrambled to leave the building. This change in events gave John a sense of grim satisfaction. In the chaos of everyone scrambling to leave, John noted one very large man step forward. The man was not quite as tall as

John, however, he outweighed John by a large margin. He was not a fat man either, he was entirely muscle. As he stepped forward John could see the bands of muscle move on his body. His arms were as big around as John's head, and his legs were even bigger still.

"It will be a pleasure crushing you to dust." The man said in a deep, Russian voice.

"Whatever you say, Ivan." John said in a mocking tone. John did not know the man's name, but he did not think he was far off.

In his Russian accent the man said, "My name is not Ivan."

"Well then, please enlighten me, I prefer to know the names of the people I kill." John retorted.

The man chuckled to himself. His laugh sounded more like the growl of a bear than a laugh, but the smile upon his face betrayed the sound of anger. "My name is Igor, and I am going to kill you."

"Well Igor, quit talking and make a move." John said.

Igor advanced slowly, squeezing his hands in a repetitive motion. As Igor moved closer John was paying attention to everything, trying to figure out a weakness. He knew that sheer strength was not going to help him here. He was going to have to be more cunning than the man. John looked around to see if there was anything around him that might lend him assistance. As he glanced about, his eyes fell on the knives that the last group had. He decided that was his only option, however, he would need to drag the fight out a little bit in order to get to the knives. John was too busy looking around to realize that Igor had rushed him. The speed at which the man moved surprised John. He was barely able to move out of the way as Igor threw a punch. Johns heartbeat doubled and the near miss made him reevaluate his fighting method. Igor recovered quickly, and turned to face John once more. John silently cursed himself, as Igor was now between him and the knives. By the man's speed John now knew that drawing his 1911 was going to be near impossible. He didn't think it a likely action in the first place, but now he entirely discounted the idea.

John stood and waited for Igor to make another move. He needed Igor to rush at him again so that he could get closer to the knives. John did not have to wait very long. Igor rushed him once more and this time came even closer to succeeding in catching John. The air in front of John's face seemed to vibrate due to the immensity and speed of Igor's fist. The attack allowed John to slide past Igor and reach the knives. He quickly picked up one in each hand, and tested the weight. He wanted to make sure they would not throw off his movements too much. Satisfied with them, John now moved toward Igor, intending to go on the offensive. Igor threw another punch, which John stepped inside of, and rotating he used the knife in his right hand to slash at Igor's arm. The blade bit into the flesh right below Igor's elbow and drew a jagged line nearly to his wrist before coming out of his arm at an angle. Igor howled from the slice as John twisted, and with the other blade, cut open a large whole in Igor's right rib cage. With the two attacks Igor stumbled from the pain, however, he manager to stay on his feet. As Igor turned to face John again, John could see the pain and anger in his face. John realized that although he may have dealt two nasty wounds to Igor, he had not even begun to stop him. Igor advanced at John even faster now. He acted like he was going to throw a punch with his left arm, and as John acted to repeat his last move, Igor swung at his ribs. John realized his mistake too late and swore as Igor's fist drove home. Stars sprung into life in John's eyes as Igor's fist broke several ribs. Before John realized what was happening, he landed on his back and his head hit the floor with a painful thud. John saw more stars as his vision threatened to black out. Just as John was regaining his vision, he saw a pair of massive hands reach down and grab the front of his shirt. Then he was being lifted off the ground. He hung like a limp shirt as Igor held onto him. His broken ribs causing him pain with every breath. John was surprised to realize he still had the knife in his right hand. He could tell Igor had either not noticed it, or didn't care. He was looking John in the eyes and saying something that John barely caught. "You will pay for the cuts you gave me. I will make your death extra painful." Igor said in his accent. John took the moment in and thrust his right arm forward, hoping to catch Igor off guard. His felt the knife sink home in Igor's throat. Surprise flashed across Igor's face. Igor let go of the shirt he was holding and John collapsed on the floor. Igor stumbled back as realization flashed on his face. Then Igor did the worst thing he could've and pulled the knife free, as he did, blood gushed out of the hole in his neck. Igor looked at John and tried to say something, but only managed to gurgle before falling forward on his face.

CHAPTER 28

John sat on the floor where Igor dropped him, rubbing his neck. *Damn that was close,* He thought. John looked around, and there were no more of Franks men for him to contend with. He did not understand why, but the rest of them had run. He figured that maybe the men were only supposed to keep him busy, although it definitely seemed as though they were trying to kill him. His left leg throbbed and there was still blood seeping out of it at an alarming rate. John looked around and ripped some cloth from one of the shirts of the bodies near him. He tied the strip around his leg as carefully as he could. He paused for a moment and then quickly cinched the fabric down. As tough as John was, he wasn't able to keep a moan of pain from escaping his lips. Luckily the would had been on the outside of his leg and thus the bullet had gone through and through. This meant there was nothing to dig out.

Slowly, John got to his feet. His leg hurt, and threatened not to support him. After standing for a few seconds, and leaning against the railing next to him, John was able to get his leg to cooperate. John picked up his pistol from where he had dropped it when Igor came after him. Then he picked his way through the bodies back to where his M4 lay on the ground. Picking up the M4, John released the magazine and let it clatter to the floor. Then he pulled a fresh one from his pocket and slammed it home. He checked the bolt to make sure a round was still in the chamber, which there was. He then checked the 1911 to make sure it was loaded, and began to pick his way to the stairs.

John wasn't sure where Frank had gone with Lane, but he was certain that the man was still in the building. This was his master trap, which meant he would be waiting for John somewhere. John slowly descended the stairs, with his leg throbbing with every step. When he got to the bottom he looked around to see if anything looked suspicious. John had seen Frank run toward the back of the building and thus decided to move that way. Walking to the back of the building, he looked around to see if anything was out of the ordinary. As he was scanning his surroundings, John noticed what appeared to be a staircase descending into the ground. *That has to be it*, he thought. John let the rifle hang loosely from his torso via the sling and pulled the 1911 out of its holster. Then he began to slowly descend the stairs. At the bottom of the stairs he came to a closed door with a camera above it. The camera moved a little, and then the door started to swing inward. As it did John saw the horror of the situation that he was now in. Kneeling on the plush rug in front of a desk were both Lane and Kyle. Frank stood over Kyle, and another man stood over Lane. Both had weapons trained on the two. John made a move to bring his 1911 to bear, and heard Frank utter a disapproving sound.

"You may wish to rethink what you are about to do John." Frank said in a deceptively calm voice. John let his hand fall to his side and rest there.

"That's a good boy John. Here I thought it was going to take a little more persuading to get you to give up." As Frank said this he pushed the end of the pistol he was holding against Kyle's head.

John could feel his emotions faltering, but he managed to hold it together. Looked Frank in the eyes, John said with as much hate as he could manage, "I.. AM.. GOING.. TO.. KILL.. YOU." He said it with such conviction, he saw that it made Frank readjust his grip. John could tell the man was afraid of what he was capable of. John had single handedly taken out over a hundred of Franks men.

Frank looked at John, "One more word from your mouth, and Chris here will end poor little Lane's life right in front of you. Then I will end your friend here. And you will have nothing left to live for. I do not let people go against my will John. What you have done, is the biggest betrayal I have ever suffered from someone. You don't deserve to live. And after I have taken everything from you, I will keep you as a pet. To let you wallow in your depression till you die of old age. There is no winning for you. You may be a fine killer, but if you move in a threatening manner at all, both your son and your best friend here will perish. So drop the weapon, and kneel, or they both die."

John thought about his options, and he looked from Lane to Kyle. Lane was crying silently, and Kyle was looking him in the eyes. As the two met eyes, Kyle made a very subtle motion. He looked down at the ground in front of him and then shook his head ever so slightly. John understood the motion. He couldn't give up. When he gave up, Frank would probably kill Lane and Kyle anyway. There was no negotiating with this man, and there was no winning. John knew he had to take a chance. He knew that he could shoot one man before he fired, but was not certain in his ability to shoot the second. He looked at Kyle one more time, and Kyle looked toward Lane. John knew that Kyle wanted John to shoot Chris first. All of this took place in only a matter of a couple of seconds.

"What's it going to be John." Frank said in a flat tone.

John closed his eyes and slowly nodded his head, and when he opened his eyes. He moved with all of the speed he was capable, and fired one round at Chris. The man didn't even know what happened before the bullet exited the back of his skull. After the first shot John quickly tried to aim at Frank. But before he could, John heard another gunshot. John watched as Kyle slumped forward from Franks shot. Then John brought his gun to bear on Frank. Frank just grinned, "You were too slow boy." Then John shot him.

CHAPTER 29

John ran up to where Kyle lay on the floor and tried to roll him over to see if he could save his life. However, John saw that there would be no saving Kyle, as the bullet had passed through his head. John then looked at Lane, and saw that his son was unharmed. John ran over to the boy, who's eyes were streaming with tears. John picked him up and started to comfort him. The entire time, John stared at Kyle's body, feeling tears well up. John felt as though he had failed Kyle. He suddenly started to get angry that he wasn't fast enough to shoot both men before they fired. John felt, rather than heard Lane try to snap him out of his fog. Lane was pulling on his shirt. "Daddy, please... Daddy, can we please leave?"

"Of course lane. Daddy just needs to get his friend."

John set Lane down, and walked over to where Kyle's body lay. John gingerly rolled Kyle's body over, and picked it up. With Kyle in his arms, John walked with Lane up the stairs. When they reached the top of the stairs, John turned and took Lane back to the SUV he had shown up in. It was beat up but was still running. John had Lane help him get rear hatch open, and he carefully loaded Kyle's body in the back. After John and Lane got into the SUV, he took off down a side street. John knew he was going to have to get out of sight, and out of the area pretty quickly. They had created a lot of noise, and he knew that the authorities would be on their way soon. John drove for what seemed like ages. He was trying to figure out what he was going to do about Kyle. What he decided to do was going to be difficult to do without getting caught, but he wanted to make sure that Kyle got the Hero's burial he deserved. John drove till he found a funeral home. He went inside, leaving Lane in the SUV, and came back out with a simple wooden casket. He had also managed to grab some paper and a pen.

John then drove to a part of town where he wouldn't be noticed. When he stopped, John got out and loaded Kyle into the box. With a handwritten note. Then he loaded up the box and left again.

Lane still hadn't said anything other than when he had spoken at the warehouse. John knew that he would come around in his own time. John understood that his son had gone through a very traumatic set of events, and so he needed time. The next step in John's process was the hardest. He was going to have to wait till after the day shift went home, so there would be less people at the precinct. John took the SUV to a random part of town, and him and Lane sat in silence for the better part of the day. They left the spot only once to go get food and then returned.

At 11 pm John slowly pulled up to the precinct. He needed to make sure he was fast and not seen other than where he was going to leave Kyle. John backed up the SUV close to the edge of where he knew there was a blind spot in the cameras. He then unloaded Kyle's box, and slowly pushed it to where the camera could see it. As he did, John let tears run down his face. "I'm sorry that I failed you my friend. The halls of Valhalla wait for a warrior as fierce as yourself." Then John got back into the SUV and left.

CHAPTER 30

After dropping off the box, John immediately headed to the airport. There was a small window of time in which he and Lane would be able to leave the US without being stopped. John had hoped that the precinct hadn't seen fit to ground all of his aliases. When John got to the airport, he bought the tickets and was relieved when the Alias he had chosen wasn't questioned. He would fly to Switzerland where he and Lane could build his new life. John was tense the entire time as him and Lane waited to board their flight. However, he was not stopped or challenged as he boarded the plane. When the plane took off, John breathed a sigh of relief, holding onto Lane very tightly.

John sat in the window plane seat above the clouds and thought about the note that he had left with Kyle. He hoped it would be enough, but he knew that there was no telling how the precinct would respond.

The Note read: "Here Lies Kyle Grafton, the best friend, partner and detective I have ever known. I am sorry to leave him here with this note, but I will not be turning myself in. Kyle only did what he thought was right by helping me. He died protecting my son and thus he will always be the hero to whom my son and myself owe our lives. As you may well know by now, Frank "The Crusher" Johnson has been eliminated. Kyle deserves a hero's burial and I do hope he gets that. Please liquidate everything I own and make sure his next of Kin is taken care of. I was the only family that I know that Kyle had, but please make sure that everything I have is used to care for him. Kyle Grafton is and always will be a Hero."

John smiled in spite of the tears, and knew that Kyle would get the Hero's burial he deserved. That was the only consolation he was going to receive, and that had to be enough.

EPILOGUE

Captain Hormel sat in a low backed chair and watched as the workers lowered the casket into the ground. He was angry and sad at the same time. He didn't know what to do with his feelings. The mess that John had left behind had been enormous. However, at the same time, John had taken out the single biggest criminal in Miami. John had done him a favor, but that wasn't how it was being portrayed. The media had spun it sideways, of course. They said that a rogue detective had gone on a murdering spree, taking out another detective in the way. Hormel had decided to leave the media to their devices. He knew that if anyone in the media knew the truth, Kyle wouldn't get the hero's burial he deserved. He was so damn angry at Kyle and John, because they were his two best detectives. They had both gone AWOL, and ended up with one dead, and the other presumably fleeing the country.

After the casket was lowered into the ground and everyone had said their peace. The congregation broke up and people began to leave. Captain Hormel walked back to his car, to head back to the precinct. As he was walking, more media personnel accosted him. Asking him question after question. "Did you help John." "Do you know where John is." When he finally got to his car and opened the door, Hormel turned around and simply said, "I decline to answer any further questions. Then he got in the car and shut the door.

About half an hour later, Hormel showed back up to the precinct. He walked into his office, and sat in his chair. It was only 10 am, but he was exhausted.

He leaned back and closed his eyes for a moment. He took a deep breath, and then leaned forward to begin the days work. When he opened his eyes, he noticed a postcard sitting on his desk. There was no return label, and it was definitely from another country. By the picture, it looked as though it was from somewhere in Europe. There were white capped mountains, and a sun in the background looking much too large. He stared at it for a moment, and then flipped it over. On the back there was something written.

"Captain, I am sorry for the mess. It was necessary. I was able to rescue Lane. And we are safe. Many regards. -J"

www.ingramcontent.com/pod-product-compliance
Lightning Source LLC
Chambersburg PA
CBHW071927130726
47909CB00014B/2612